DARK ALLEY DECEPTION

Mr. Rawley and his stepsons turned toward the black car expectantly.

But nobody expected what came next.

Two men jumped out of the black car. They tore the briefcase out of Walter Rawley's hand and hustled Greg and Mike at gunpoint into the back seat of the car. Walter Rawley stood empty-handed and open-mouthed as the car roared off.

In the alley, Frank and Joe and the others stood openmouthed too.

Linda Rawley found her voice first.

"You were all wrong," she whispered. "Dead wrong!"

Books in THE HARDY BOYS CASEFILES® Series

Available from ARCHWAY Paperbacks

THE HARDY BOYS CASEFILES NO. 15

BLOOD RELATIONS

FRANKLIN W. DIXON

AN ARCHWAY PAPERBACK
Published by POCKET BOOKS
New York   London   Toronto   Sydney   Tokyo

AN ARCHWAY PAPERBACK *Original*

An Archway Paperback published by
POCKET BOOKS, a division of Simon & Schuster, Inc.
1230 Avenue of the Americas, New York, N.Y. 10020

ISBN: 0-671-64461-0

First Archway Paperback printing May 1988

10 9 8 7 6 5 4 3 2 1

THE HARDY BOYS, AN ARCHWAY PAPERBACK and
colophon are registered trademarks of Simon & Schuster, Inc.

THE HARDY BOYS CASEFILES is a trademark
of Simon & Schuster, Inc.

Printed in the U.S.A.

IL 7+

BLOOD RELATIONS

Chapter
1

"YOU'RE WRONG—*DEAD* wrong," Callie Shaw snapped at Frank Hardy as they crossed the Bayport Mall parking lot after school. They were heading toward Mr. Pizza. "I happen to think Greg Rawley is a nice guy. That's no reason for you to get jealous."

"Jealous?" Frank answered indignantly, starting to walk in front of a moving car and being snatched back just in time by Callie. "All I'm saying is we really don't know much about Greg—or his brother Mike, for that matter. They *seem* okay, but everybody knows they spent a year on their own and nobody knows what they did then. That's all I meant."

He held the door of the pizza parlor open for Callie. She suppressed a smile as she brushed her

1

long blond mane back and breezed coolly past him.

"Come on, Frank," she said as they sat at a corner table. "You look like somebody just rained on your parade. When they showed up in school this year, you said that the only thing wrong with them was they were too straight. And now, just because I happen to admit that I think Greg's nice, not to mention cute, you decide he's a so-called suspicious character."

Frank narrowed his dark eyes and opened his mouth as if to argue further, but decided he couldn't. Callie was being logical, and logic was one thing that Frank Hardy never argued with. "I'll get the pizza," he said.

"I have to admit," Frank continued when he returned to the table with sodas and a medium pie loaded with pepperoni and mushrooms—Callie's favorite, "I do tend to see suspicious characters everywhere. It kind of comes with the territory."

Callie, who now and then helped the Hardy brothers out with their detective work, nodded in agreement. "You show definite signs of burnout," she said. "Good thing you and Joe don't have any cases right now."

"Yeah, it's good to have time off," said Frank. "I'm going to work out some new programs for my computer. Phil Cohen's going to help. He's the only guy I know who's a bigger hacker than I am."

"What about Joe?" Callie asked.

"He doesn't mind taking a break from work either. He figures this is going to be his year as Bayport's star running back, and he's training extra hard."

"Speak of the devil, here he comes now," Callie said. Frank followed her gaze to see his younger brother enter the restaurant. With Joe was his teammate and pal, Biff Hooper. Although Joe was six feet tall and solidly built, he seemed almost fragile next to Biff, a fullback who looked like a human bulldozer and played like one, too.

"How did practice go?" Frank asked when they joined Callie and him at the table.

"Great," said Biff. "This is going to be a championship year." He grinned at Joe. "Especially with the big surprise we got today. Right, Joe?"

"Yeah, a great big surprise," said Joe, brushing a hand through his short blond hair. He didn't sound happy.

"What happened?" asked Callie.

"What happened was that Mike Rawley tried out for the team," said Biff. "And he's good. Really good. Right, Joe?"

"He's okay," said Joe grudgingly, helping himself to a slice of the pizza. "Kind of flashy, but, yeah, he's okay. I mean, it's hard to know how he'd stand up to any punishment, but on the surface he's not bad.''

"What position's he trying out for?" asked Callie, her eyes lighting up. "Wait. Don't tell me. Let me guess. It wouldn't be running back, would it? He wouldn't be competition for you, would he, Joe?"

Callie sat back and grinned while Joe squirmed. Callie liked Joe, of course, but she didn't mind needling him once in a while. As far as she was concerned, it kept his cockiness from getting out of control.

"Competition? For me? No way," Joe said, grinning. "Maybe the coach can use him to give me a rest after one of my touchdown runs."

"You might get to have a rest and sit out the *whole* game if Mike keeps showing the speed he showed today," said Biff, winking at Callie.

"I'm not so sure about that," said Joe defensively. "I watched him pretty closely, and I noticed he was really puffing toward the end of the session."

"Honestly, you're even worse than Frank," said Callie. "Why won't you two give the Rawley brothers a chance?"

"Callie's right, Joe," Frank chimed in. "We have to be fair to them. I mean, they just moved to Bayport and started a new school, and they've handled it really well. They've been friendly but not too pushy, and it only took them a couple of weeks to start being part of the crowd. You have to agree, basically they're okay."

Joe nodded. "Yeah, you're right." Then he grinned. "But I'm not going to roll over and play dead for Mike. No way is he beating me out."

Biff glanced at his watch. "Let's split another pizza before I go home and hit the books. If I blow my test, the coach'll bench me."

"Right," said Joe. A speculative look came into his eyes. "I wonder how Mike's doing in *his* classes."

"Ask him," Callie suggested. "Here he comes now—with Greg."

It was easy to spot Greg and Mike Rawley the moment they walked into the pizza parlor. Both of them had short flame-red hair. Other than their hair, they blended in well with the preppie crowd, even though their jeans were a little less faded and more sharply pressed than most, their shirts less wrinkled, their windbreakers better fitting, and their loafers less scuffed. Both of them were a little over six feet tall, practically the same height as Frank and Joe. Their ages were the same as the Hardys, too: Greg, eighteen, Mike a year younger.

Callie started to wave to get their attention, then saw she didn't have to. They had already spotted their table and were making a beeline for it.

Frank, perhaps a little guiltily, gave them an

extra-warm greeting. "Hey, guys, come on and sit down. Plenty of room."

"Yeah, we can order a super-pizza special," Joe said. "I figure you can use a couple of slices, Mike. You really put it out on the field today."

But Greg and Mike didn't respond to the friendly welcome, nor to the big smile that Callie flashed them. Their faces were serious, almost grim. So were their voices.

Although Greg did say hello to everyone at the table, his attention was only on the Hardys. "Frank, Joe, we were hoping to find you here. We called your house and your aunt Gertrude said you weren't home yet," said Mike. "So we figured we'd check here."

"Good thinking," said Frank, flicking his dark brown hair back in place. "Mr. Pizza is our home away from home."

"What did you want to see us about?" asked Joe.

Greg cleared his throat and glanced at the others at the table. "It's, uh, kind of private."

"I know when I'm not wanted," said Callie.

"It's not that, Callie," Greg said hastily. Frank had to suppress a twinge of anger as Greg looked deep into Callie's eyes. Frank noticed that she didn't look away. "It's just that, well, you know . . ." Greg said to her, letting his voice trail off apologetically.

"I was only teasing," Callie said. "I have to be going anyway."

"I'll head out with you," Biff said.

"Look, no hard feelings," Mike said quickly.

"No problem," Biff said good-naturedly. "People are always coming to Frank and Joe with their troubles. I'll just say good luck and get out of here."

After Callie and Biff left, Greg and Mike took their places. Both sat on the edge of their seats.

"I hope you're not too busy to help us," Greg said.

"We don't want to impose," said Mike.

"Don't worry. Whatever it is, we'll do everything we can to help," said Frank in a relaxed voice, trying to put them at ease.

Joe said with a grin, "Sure. You can count on us. No trouble too big or too small."

But his grin faded when he heard Greg say, "This trouble is big."

"Come on, Greg," said Joe. "You make it sound like a matter of life or death."

"It *is* a matter of life or death," Greg said grimly.

Chapter

2

GREG AND MIKE Rawley had arrived in Bayport a week before school started. Except that their last name hadn't been Rawley then. It was Jones, the same name their mother had before she married Walter P. Rawley. But they had taken the last name of their stepfather as soon as they moved into his house with their mother, now Linda Rawley. As soon as Greg and Mike settled in, Walter Rawley legally changed their last name to his.

Walter had been happy to do it. He and his first wife had had no children. After her death in a car accident, he had lived alone for three years. Then he had met the boys' mother on a business trip to California and brought her to Bayport as his bride.

Greg and Mike hadn't come to Bayport with the Rawleys. In fact, they hadn't even known their mother remarried.

As Greg once explained it to Frank, Joe, and Callie, sitting outside in the warm September sun during a school lunch break, "My dad died in an airplane crash a year and a half ago. That was a really bad time—our family was totally ripped apart. My mom took it hard and she pretty much lost interest in everything. As for Mike and me, all we wanted to do was get away from our house and all the memories of how happy our lives had been. So we stuffed what we could in our backpacks, laced up our hiking boots, and started thumbing around the country. We used to drop our mom postcards every now and then, but for almost a year, we were off on our own."

"We saw a lot of America," Mike had said. "Parts of Canada and Mexico too. In fact, we were thinking of getting jobs on a boat going to Europe and then to the Middle East. But when we called home to tell Mom about it, we got her Bayport phone number. She told us she had married again. And you know, we suddenly decided we didn't want to see any more of the world. What we wanted to see was Mom again, stay at home, and get our lives back on track."

"Mr. Rawley's been great to us, he's given us a lot of help," Greg had said warmly. "He really went to bat for us with the school to let us make up courses rather than being dropped back a grade.''

"And when he gave us his name, it was like we were a real family again," Mike had said. "He didn't have to do that. We weren't part of the deal when he married Mom. As far as she was concerned, we were gone for good. That's what she told Mr. Raw—I mean, Dad, he wants us to call him that—when they first got to know each other."

"So it must have been kind of a surprise to him when you suddenly showed up," Frank said.

"It had to be," Greg agreed. "But he didn't let it bother him. He accepted us from the day we walked in the door."

"It sure was a relief to us," Mike had said. "Not to mention how good it made Mom feel."

Greg nodded. "Practically the first thing she told us, after she saw how great Mr. Raw—I mean, Dad—was being about it, was that the one big worry she had was gone. Now she was free to be perfectly happy."

That was the story Greg and Mike had told the Hardys a little more than a week before. But now, sitting at the table with Frank and Joe at Mr. Pizza, their story was different.

"Mom is scared," Greg said, his voice wire-tight, his knuckles showing white as his hands clenched on the tabletop.

"She's scared to death," Mike echoed.

"Of what?" asked Frank.

"We're not sure," said Greg.

"But we have an idea," said Mike. He stopped, clearly reluctant to go further.

"What do you know?" asked Frank.

"Who's your mom afraid of?" asked Joe.

Greg opened his mouth, then closed it. He opened it again, and managed to get one word out: "Dad."

"Dad?" repeated Frank, shaking his head in shock.

"You mean, your real dad, don't you?" said Joe, trying to make sense of their statement. "You don't mean Mr. Rawley. You can't mean him."

"Our real dad is dead," said Greg. "Mom isn't afraid of ghosts."

"But Mr. Rawley?" Frank asked, still incredulous.

"I know it sounds crazy," said Greg. "In fact, I hope it is crazy. Except that would make Mom crazy, and I don't want that either."

"Maybe you should start from the beginning and tell us what you're talking about," said Frank.

"And it had better be good, if you expect us to believe you," Joe added.

Joe meant what he said, and he was talking for Frank as well. Walter Rawley was one of the wealthiest men in Bayport, the founder, presi-

11

dent, and chief stockholder of Laser, Inc., an electronics company that had become a spectacular success because of its bold research and advance technology. Walter Rawley didn't just contribute money to local charities, he gave his time too.

But the key fact was that Walter Rawley was an old friend of their father, Fenton Hardy, and Joe and Frank had known him since they were little kids. As far as Joe and Frank were concerned, Walter Rawley was a good guy. And it would take a lot to make them think of him any other way.

"A couple of days ago, Mom started acting nervous. I know that that doesn't sound like much, but you had to see the way she looked to understand," Mike said. "It was like she was terrified every time Dad walked into the room. She tried to hide it, but couldn't."

Greg took over, glancing worriedly at his brother. "I don't know if Dad noticed, but Greg and I did because—well, she's our mom and we know her so well."

"Did you talk to her about it?" asked Frank.

"It was hard because we didn't know what was going on with her and Dad—but we did," said Greg.

"And she said?" Frank asked.

"That we were imagining things. That there was nothing wrong," said Mike. "But the way she looked and sounded when she said it convinced us we were right. Something really was wrong."

Greg picked up the story. "We both felt as if she was protecting us from something. And a day later we found out what it was."

"I went to her room to tell her we were going out. She was sitting there reading a little red book and crying," Mike said. "She tried to hide it and stop crying as soon as she saw me, but she realized that it was too late."

"By that time I had come upstairs," Greg said. "She made both of us promise that we would never mention that book to anyone. Especially Dad."

"What was in the book?" asked Frank. "You must have asked her that."

"We did," Mike retorted. "But she wouldn't tell us. She just said that if we wanted her marriage to survive we had to keep her secret."

"She said it was better that we didn't know," said Greg. "But what really scared us was when she said that it was *safer* if we didn't know what was in the book."

"Do you know what she did with the book?" asked Joe. "Is there any way you can get your hands on it?"

"That's why we came to you," said Greg. "We know where the book is, but we can't get it, not without your help."

13

"What kind of help?" asked Frank, even though he could guess what was coming.

"Callie and some of the other kids told us about your detective work," said Greg. "They didn't give us a whole lot of details, but from what they said we felt pretty sure you two know how to get at things that are locked up. I hope we're right."

Frank and Joe exchanged glances. The Rawley brothers were right. The boys had picked up a number of skills that most people would think were more appropriate for criminals than detectives. Among those skills were lock-picking and safecracking. The question Frank and Joe were asking themselves was whether or not to use them now?

"Are you sure you don't want to try talking to your mother again?" Frank asked.

"You don't understand *how* scared she was, Frank," Greg replied. "I think something in that book has convinced her that her life is in danger—in danger from my stepfather. And I think it has something to do with the way his first wife died."

"And don't tell us to go to the police," Mike said heatedly. "We know we don't have any evidence, and anyway, they'd have to talk to our stepfather and that's just what Mom's most afraid of."

"You're right about the police," Frank acknowledged. "They do prefer hard evidence, rather than simple suspicion."

"You've got to help us, guys," Greg said. "Think if it were your own mother. What would you do?"

Again Frank and Joe glanced at each other. Joe coughed uneasily.

"I have to say that as much as I respect Mr. Rawley, this situation is strange enough to interest me," Frank said carefully.

"Don't let him kid you, guys." Joe grinned. "We haven't had any action in a while and Frank's scared of getting rusty. But seriously," he continued, "where is this lock you need us to open and when can we get at it?"

"Then you'll do it?" Greg asked eagerly.

"The way you put it, I don't see how we can say no," said Frank, and Joe nodded in agreement. "Only thing is, you'll have to check the inside of the safe. We can't do that."

"Great," said Greg.

"We don't know how to thank you," said Mike.

"You don't have to thank us," said Frank. "Just get us into the house and point us in the right direction."

At eleven-thirty that night, when the Hardys knocked on the back door of the Rawley house, everything seemed as if it would go perfectly. Mr.

and Mrs. Rawley had gone into New York City to have dinner and see a play. They weren't expected back until after midnight.

Frank and Joe had told their parents they were going to bed early, then had slipped down the back stairs and out of the house. They had ridden their bikes to the Rawleys' rather than wake anyone by starting up their van.

The Rawley house was one of the largest in its neighborhood—one of the most exclusive sections of town. Although the streets were deserted, the boys coasted silently down the driveway to the Rawley house. Then they quickly dismounted and walked their bikes around to the back of the house.

The back door was opened quickly after they knocked. The brothers slipped in, and Greg reached for the light switch. But Frank shook his head, snapping on a flashlight instead and keeping the beam on the floor.

"You really are cautious," said Greg as he led the way out of the large kitchen they had entered.

"Better safe than sorry," answered Frank.

The Hardys followed Greg across the living room to a set of wide stairs. "It's been redecorated since we were here last," Joe said with a hint of fondness in his voice.

"You've been here before?" Mike asked.

"Yeah. Before Mr. Rawley's first wife died. He

kind of changed after that, and we hardly saw him," Joe answered.

"We've only met your mother once," Frank said as they climbed the stairs and entered a luxurious blue and white bedroom. "We bumped into her with Mr. Rawley at the mall."

"I'll show you what you have to open," said Greg.

He led them to a large walk-in closet and slid the clothes out of the way, revealing a small wall safe at the back.

"How did you find the hiding place?" Frank asked.

"I really hate to admit this—we searched everywhere, and this is the only place it could be," said Greg sheepishly.

"It felt lousy to do it," Mike added, "but we had to. Do you think you can get into this?"

"Sure," Frank said confidently as he unloaded what looked like a stethoscope tipped with a suction cup, a tiny but very complicated calculator, and an assortment of lock picks from his pockets. While he was eyeing the door of the safe, Joe flicked on another flashlight and began searching the rest of the closet.

"Hey, what are you doing?" Greg asked.

Frank cut him off. "Almost everybody who has a safe figures that sooner or later he's going to forget the combination. So he writes it down somewhere. Sometimes you can get lucky and find it.''

''I'm coming up empty,'' Joe said.

''So then it's probably a number they'll always remember. We just have to outthink your mom,'' said Frank. ''When did your mom and stepfather get married?''

''October twenty-third of last year,'' said Greg. ''Why?''

Frank held up a hand to cut him off. ''Right, twenty-three, left and—''

The click of the safe's tumblers was audible to all four boys. Frank reached for the handle to open the safe door and at that moment a beam from another flashlight froze the boys in place.

''Don't move. Or you're dead!''

Chapter

3

FRANK TURNED TO look but he was blinded by the white glare.

"Pull down the shades," the voice commanded.

After Greg pulled them down, the overhead light came on in the room.

Facing them was a hard-faced man in a trench coat, holding a nickel-plated .45 automatic that looked as big as a cannon.

"Stay close together and put your hands on your heads," said the man. "Don't even think of trying any funny business. This forty-five holds seven rounds, and I'd need only four for you punks.

"Now, we can have a little conversation. Tell me sweet and simple, who told you to break in here? And what do you know about the other plans?"

"Look, man, I don't know who you think you are, but you've got us wrong," Greg said.

"Yeah, we didn't break in," said Mike. "We live here. I'm Mike Rawley; this is my brother Greg; and these are our friends Frank and Joe Hardy. You're making a big mistake."

"You're the ones making a mistake if you expect me to swallow that story." The man sneered. "I'm supposed to believe you're breaking into your parents' safe? Let's try again."

"Look, my brother and I have identification," said Greg, desperate. "At least take a look at it."

The man considered for a moment. Then he said grudgingly, "Okay, I'll take a look. But I want you to move real slow. One at a time, very slowly take out your wallets and toss them so they land at my feet. Remember you make one quick move, and it'll be your last."

Greg, then Mike, did as told. Keeping his gun leveled on his prisoners, the man bent down and picked up the wallets, pulling out the IDs.

"These *look* okay," he said. "But you still have some explaining to do. What were you kids doing here tonight?"

"We were worried about our mom," Greg said. "She's been scared of something lately, and she won't say what. But we know it has something to do with a little book she locked in the safe with her jewelry. We wanted to get a look at it and find out what's bothering her."

Before the man could speak, Joe interrupted him. "Hey, don't you want to see my ID?" Joe asked.

"And mine?" said Frank.

The Hardys slowly lowered their hands to their pockets. Then they moved fast.

Both pulled out rings of keys and simultaneously fired them at the man.

As he ducked, Joe hit him with a diving tackle around the knees.

By the time the stranger shook the cobwebs from his head and staggered to his feet, his gun was in Frank's hand.

"We had to do it," Joe explained to Greg and Mike. "We didn't want you to tell this guy anything more."

"And you'd already told him too much," Frank said, elaborating. "All we know is that he's not a policeman. And he *was* sneaking around your mother's bedroom with a gun."

Both Greg and Mike turned pale.

"Now it's our turn to ask some questions," Joe said.

Frank held the gun steady on the man. "Your turn to produce some ID, pal. And as you said to us, no tricks."

"Hey, don't get crazy," the man said nervously. "Those things have a tendency to go off when you don't want them to. And that one has a sensitive trigger."

"Uh, I don't know much about these things," said Frank, fumbling with the .45 as if he had never held a gun before.

Both Frank and Joe were expert marksmen, but they had promised their father they'd never carry firearms.

"Look, kid, just be careful with that thing and I'll tell you whatever you want to know," the man said. "I'll just sit here. You ask and I'll answer."

Frank nodded. "Let's see that ID, slowly, and no tricks. Toss it to my brother."

The man moved cautiously, never taking his eyes off the gun in Frank's hand. With elaborate slowness he pulled out his wallet and tossed it to Joe.

Joe opened it, pulled out a business card, and read, " 'John Dunn. Licensed private investigator. Security is my specialty.' "

"My license is in there too," Dunn insisted.

Joe pulled it out, looked it over, and said, "It looks authentic enough, though you never can tell."

"Okay, we've seen your ID," said Frank. "Now let's hear your explanation of what *you* were doing here. Who hired you? And why?"

"Mrs. Rawley hired me to make sure nobody took that book. She said if the wrong person found out what was in there, it could cost her her life.''

There was a chilling silence.

Finally Greg broke it. "Tell us more."

"Yeah," said Mike. "Who was she afraid of?"

"She made me swear not to reveal that," Dunn said. "She said she wasn't sure what she thought was true, and she couldn't do anything until she got real proof."

"Come on, she's our mother, you have to tell us," Greg pleaded.

"No," Dunn said. "I gave her my word."

"That may be true," said Frank. "But right now I think we can answer a lot more questions by taking a look at this book for ourselves."

He passed the gun to his brother, clicking the safety on as he did so. It took only a moment for him to step back into the closet and open the safe.

Greg stepped in and looked. "It's empty," he managed to choke out.

"It means that your mother's worst fears have come true," said Dunn, interrupting. "Somebody has gotten into the safe and found her book."

"Maybe Mom took it with her," Mike said. "She could have done that, couldn't she?"

"She wanted me here tonight," Dunn replied, "because the book was here."

"Somebody must have gotten into the safe before we did," Frank said.

23

"And I think I know who that person was," Dunn said.

"Who?" said Greg urgently. "You have to tell us."

Dunn had opened his mouth to answer when a voice shouting from downstairs made him stop.

"Greg! Mike! You home? Come here right away!"

"Dad," Greg said.

"They must have come home right after the show," Mike said.

"Greg! Mike!" the voice shouted again, this time even louder. It was closer too. Mr. Rawley was heading toward the stairs.

"Quick, into my room," Greg said in a whisper.

With Greg and Mike leading the way, Frank, Joe, and Dunn dashed out of the room down the hall and into Greg's closet. Greg and Mike flipped on the stereo and sat down at a large desk piled high with books.

In the dark, the Hardys and Dunn concentrated on listening.

"Come in!" Greg shouted in response to a knock.

"Didn't you hear me? I was shouting for you," said Mr. Rawley.

"Sorry, Dad," said Mike. "Greg and I were cramming for a test tomorrow, and besides, we had the stereo on."

"What's up?" asked Greg. "You look like something's wrong."

"Something is wrong, very wrong," said Mr. Rawley. "You'd better brace yourselves for a shock."

"A shock?" asked Mike, his voice higher pitched than usual.

"What kind of shock?" Greg asked, afraid to hear the answer.

"Your mom," Mr. Rawley said. "She's been taken!"

Chapter

4

"WHAT HAPPENED?" GREG asked.

"Let's all sit down, and I'll tell you about it."

There was a short silence as Frank, Joe, and Dunn shifted uncomfortably in the closet, waiting to hear what would come next.

"It was going to be a special night," Mr. Rawley began. "Your mom had found a new French restaurant she wanted to try, and we had tickets to a Broadway show. She wore my favorite dress—the red one—" He paused to gather himself together before continuing.

"Go on," said Mike, encouraging him.

"It was all going wonderfully," Mr. Rawley continued with apparent difficulty. "The restaurant was wonderful. Soft lighting, excellent wines. After dinner we walked the ten blocks to

Times Square. It was a beautiful evening. Plenty of people out. Lights glittering all around us.

"We attended the play—a comedy. Your mom laughed and laughed." Mr. Rawley sighed. "We decided to go downtown for a nightcap before heading home. As we were leaving the theater, a cab pulled up and stopped right in front of us. I figured it was a stroke of luck. But now I know it was no accident. It was planned."

"The cab belonged to—who? Kidnappers?" Greg asked, his voice quavering slightly.

"That's right," Mr. Rawley said. "I gave the cabbie the address, but he headed off west instead of south. When I asked him about it, he said it was a way to beat the traffic, and I believed him—until he stopped the cab at a deserted spot on Tenth Avenue. A man stepped out of the shadows and opened the rear cab door. He yanked me out of the cab, handed me an envelope, got in the back seat with your mom, and the cab raced off."

"What was in the envelope?" asked Mike.

"Instructions," said Mr. Rawley, pulling a piece of paper out of his jacket pocket. " 'We have your wife. If you tell the police, we kill her fast. Don't try nothing because we will know everything you do. We stole the cab just like we stole your old lady, so you can't trace it. Keep your mouth shut and wait for us to get in touch with you if you want to see your wife alive again.

27

P.S. That goes for her kids too. They talk to anybody, and they say bye-bye to their mom.' "

There was a long silence.

Then Greg's voice: "What do we do, Dad?"

"We do exactly what we're told," said Mr. Rawley. "We wait to find out how much money they want and how they want it delivered, and I pay it to them. The money doesn't matter. But the one thing I don't intend to do is gamble with your mom's life—and I'm sure you boys don't want to either."

"Right," said Greg.

"Of course not," said Mike.

"If anybody asks where your mother is, just say she's gone to the West Coast on family business. Understand?"

There was no sound. But Frank, Joe, and Dunn, listening from the closet, knew that Greg and Mike were nodding their heads earnestly.

"Good," said Mr. Rawley. "Now, get a good night's sleep so you can appear as normal as possible in school tomorrow. It's vital that nobody suspects anything is wrong."

"Right, Dad," said Greg.

"Yeah, we understand," said Mike.

"I know I can depend on you," said Mr. Rawley. "Good night."

Frank, Joe, and Dunn heard Mr. Rawley close the room door as he left. Greg waited a minute before he opened the closet door.

"It's *him*—I know it," Greg said, his face pale, his lips thin with anger.

"He faked the kidnapping," Mike agreed. "I only hope he hasn't . . ." He couldn't make himself finish the sentence, but all of them knew what he meant.

"Hold on. Don't panic," Dunn said. "And don't jump to conclusions."

"Right," said Frank. "Remember, we don't know what your mom found in that book. Sure, it could have been your stepfather but it also could have been somebody else."

"Of course it was someone else," Joe said angrily, glaring at Greg and Mike. "I can't believe Mr. Rawley could be involved in anything like this. I've known him my entire life. You guys have only known him a couple of months, and you're accusing him of kidnapping his own wife. Maybe we ought to ask what kind of friends your mother used to have before she—"

"Lay off my mother," Greg said, stepping forward so that he and Joe stood facing each other. "She's the victim here, not that overblown con man you call your family friend."

"Yeah," Mike added. "You heard about the wicked stepmother. Well, this is the story of the wicked stepfather."

"Hold it, Joe," said Dunn, putting a hand on his arm. "All of you had better bury the hatchet right now. This ain't the time for feelings. We need facts.''

"He's right," said Frank. "We need logic, not fights.''

"You and Dunn can look for facts and logic," said Joe. "Me, I have to go with my gut feelings. I *know* Mr. Rawley is straight.''

"Your gut feelings aren't going to get Mrs. Rawley back alive," Dunn said. "Only hard work can do that. We have to work together, especially since we can't turn to the police.''

"Why not?" Greg asked, reluctantly backing off.

"For one simple reason," said Frank. "The first person the police would talk to would be Mr. Rawley. If he is one of the kidnappers, the idea that the cops might be after him would be all the reason he'd need to get rid of your mom." Frank paused when he saw Greg and Mike's reaction.

"Hey, I'm sorry to put it that way, but you have to think about the worst and hope for the best in a situation like this.''

"No apology necessary," said Greg. "We have to face facts. You're right about the police. If Mom's still alive, we don't want to make any wrong moves.''

"So what can we do?" asked Joe, getting impatient and showing it.

"Right now, not much," said Dunn. "I'm going back to New York City and nose around to see if anyone can confirm Rawley's story. But I doubt I'll have much success. Other than that, our best play is just to wait.''

"Wait?" said Greg in a pained voice.

"For what?" asked Mike.

"For the kidnappers' ransom instructions to arrive," Dunn said evenly. "The kidnappers have to tell your father how much money and when and where to deliver it. Even if Mr. Rawley isn't on the level, it has to look like a kidnapping and that means somebody has to communicate with him, tell him where to make the drop.''

Dunn handed Greg a card. "This is my home number. You can get me or my machine twenty-four hours a day. Be careful not to lose it because it's unlisted. When I'm out, I'll check in with my machine as often as I can, so phone me the minute you hear anything." He held out his hand, and Frank reluctantly handed over the .45. As soon as he pocketed the gun, Dunn said, "I'm leaving now. Check to see if the coast is clear.''

Then it was Frank and Joe's turn to leave, after arranging to meet Mike and Greg at Mr. Pizza the next day after school.

As they pedaled their bikes through the deserted one-A.M. streets of Bayport, Frank said to Joe, "It's good to have a pro like Dunn on the case.''

"I guess you're right about Dunn, though I hate to admit it," said Joe. "He seems like a real cold fish. But in this case, we can really use him and his experience. It's kind of scary to think that if we mess up, somebody dies.''

''Yeah,'' said Frank. ''Even though it's not the first time. I just wish we could talk to Dad about the case, but with him and Rawley being such close friends, we'll have to have a lot of evidence to convince him.''

Joe nodded his agreement. ''For his sake, I hope Rawley's innocent. It would really come as a shock to Dad if Rawley turned out to be a kidnapper.''

''But we also know that Dad wouldn't want us to hold back,'' said Frank. ''He's always told us not to pull punches when we go after a criminal.''

They parked their bikes and ran in through the back door.

''I've got to eat something,'' Joe said. ''There's half a roast chicken that Mom said we could eat up. Whenever we go into action, I always notice a sharp upsurge in my appetite. Some kind of law of nature, I guess.''

''A law of *your* nature, action or no action,'' said Frank. ''But I could use some chow myself. We'll split it.''

''Plus some of those brownies Aunt Gertrude baked yesterday,'' said Joe.

They were just finishing off the last of the brownies when the kitchen door slowly swung open.

Their Aunt Gertrude stood stock-still, framed in the doorway.

"Why, boys, you scared me to death. What are you doing up this time of night?" she asked. "I thought you were going to bed early."

"We were," said Frank, thinking fast. "But then Greg and Mike Rawley called us to see if we wanted to study with them for a test tomorrow."

Aunt Gertrude nodded. "Greg and Mike. I've heard they're nice boys. I was so happy to see Walter Rawley find such a sweet family. And I'm glad to see those boys are being good influences on you two. You should spend more hours on your schoolwork than you do on all those *adventures* of yours."

"And what are you doing up this late, Aunt Gertrude?" asked Joe, hoping to change the subject before she launched into her standard lecture on how they should start behaving more sensibly.

Besides, Joe already knew his aunt's answer. The late, late movies were her only vice. And the films of the forties and fifties—especially mysteries—were her absolute favorites. He knew that if he got her started talking about one of her movies, they were home free.

"Well," she said as she began making herself a cup of hot chocolate to take up to bed, "I was watching this great old thriller with—oh, he's before your time, and you wouldn't know him—

and I fell asleep just before the end and missed the climax.

"You see, a woman marries a man who seems just perfect for her. Then she discovers the diary of his first wife, who supposedly died in an accident. Reading it she finds out that the woman was afraid she was about to be murdered—and now the heroine, the second wife, has to find out if her husband is really a murderer. That's where I fell asleep."

She peered sheepishly over the rim of her cup of chocolate. "Neither of you boys knows how the movie comes out, do you?"

Joe and Frank stared at her for a long, silent moment and then at each other. Finally Frank said, "Not yet, Aunt Gertrude, but we hope to know soon. Real soon."

Chapter

5

"ANYTHING NEW?" WAS the first thing that Frank asked Greg and Mike when he and Joe met them at Mr. Pizza the next afternoon.

"Nothing," said Greg. "I called Dunn at noon to see if he'd found out anything, and he told me he'd had no luck. He had done something, though. He said he managed to put a bug on Dad's phone at the office as well as at home. He didn't want to go into details, so I didn't ask. But it might let us in on what our stepfather's up to."

"And if he's not up to anything," said Frank, "it'll let us know when the kidnappers get in touch with him. Mr. Rawley might try to keep something to himself."

Before they could discuss the matter further,

Tony Prito came over to their table. Tony, wiry, agile, and always moving, expertly juggled his life as a student at Bayport High with a good-paying job as manager of Mr. Pizza.

"Hi. How's everything?" he asked. "Just sodas today? No pizza? Want to try a slice with broccoli. It's new. I'll treat you."

"Broccoli? Sounds different," said Frank.

"Tony, you're definitely going to be the next pizza king," said Joe.

But Greg said, "Some other time. We have to be going real soon."

Frank caught his quick look and said, "Oh, yeah, I forgot. Some other time, okay?"

Tony shrugged. "Okay. But the offer won't last forever."

After Tony moved off, Joe asked, "Why do you want to cut out so fast?"

"It occurred to me that meeting here isn't a great idea," said Greg quietly. "It's too public. Why don't we meet at our house? Our stepfather's almost never there. Who knows who might be watching us and putting two and two together."

Just then, as if to prove Greg's point, Callie Shaw walked into the pizza parlor and headed straight for their table. To everyone's surprise, the grim expression on Greg's face dissolved into a smile as he watched Callie move toward them.

Frank saw his smile, and didn't like it. He told

himself he had no reason to be jealous; Callie herself had told him so too. But the way Greg looked at and talked to Callie irritated Frank.

Frank also noticed that Greg didn't seem to be in all that much of a hurry now that Callie was there.

"Hi, Callie. How's it going?" Greg said, scooting over to make room for her to sit down. "I've wanted to ask you if I could look at your physics notes. There're a couple of problems I'm not quite clear on."

"Sure," Callie said. "If you'll let me check out your French notes. There're a couple of irregular verbs I didn't get straight."

"Maybe we should have a study session sometime," Greg suggested.

This time it was Frank who said, "Hey, Greg, Joe and I are heading home. Don't you have to cut out now?"

Greg tore his eyes from Callie with obvious effort. "Oh, yeah, I almost forgot."

"Going?" Callie said. "I'll go out with you guys. I don't see anybody I feel like hanging out with, and I told Megan I'd go over to her house."

"Can I drop you off?" Greg asked.

"Sure," Callie said, surprised but obviously pleased.

"The van's outside too," Frank said. "Maybe you'd rather—"

"Rather ride in your van than our convertible?'' said Greg, grinning. ''On a nice warm September afternoon like this? No way.''

''It *is* a pretty afternoon,'' Callie said apologetically. ''And Megan's is near Greg's house. You don't mind, do you, Frank?'' She smiled sweetly at him.

''Sure, I understand,'' said Frank.

''Well, see you later,'' Greg said cheerfully as he pushed open the door and held it for Callie.

In the parking lot Frank waved, forcing a nonchalant expression on his face.

Joe was grinning as he climbed in behind the wheel. Frank slid in beside him and slammed the door.

''Say, Frank, you're not jealous, are you?'' Joe asked, his eyes twinkling. ''You don't actually think Callie would even consider throwing you over for Greg, just because he's smart, good-looking, rich, wears sharp clothes, and has a new red Porsche convertible?''

''Callie and I have an understanding. We don't have to worry about each other. We trust each other,'' huffed Frank.

''Uh-huh,'' said Joe, and his grin grew even wider as they watched Greg's convertible whiz out of the Bayport Mall ahead of them, with Greg and Callie in the front. ''You know, I find that kind of trust really beautiful. You have to tell me how you achieve it sometime.''

''Would you just drive, please,'' Frank said,

watching the convertible zoom out of sight in front of them. Greg obviously drove the Porsche as fast as he legally could.

"Don't worry about Callie, Frank," Joe said. "After we solve this case, you can tell her all about it. Remind her that you're a hero. That'll do the trick. The trouble is, you two have started to take each other for granted. That can be fatal."

"Don't be silly. Callie doesn't need a he-man bit from me. Our relationship's more mature than that," Frank said. At the same time, though, he was thinking that he just might share some of the details of this case with Callie. She might be interested to know how Greg came to him for help. Then she'd understand who needed help and who could give it when the chips were down.

When they reached the Rawley house and Frank saw again the mansion Greg lived in, he decided he'd definitely clue Callie in. After all, Callie was only human. Seeing all this wealth could turn the most level of heads.

Forty-five minutes later, still waiting in the driveway of the Rawley house, Frank wondered what Greg was doing with Callie. Probably chauffeuring her from store to store, or maybe he and Mike had invited her to have a Coke. Greg knew Frank and Joe were waiting, but from the way Greg had looked at Callie, he could have been detoured by any request or invitation Callie made.

"Wish they'd show up," Frank muttered. "We don't have all day."

"Well, you know how pretty Callie is," Joe couldn't resist saying. "Maybe Greg got distracted."

"Look, Joe, why don't you—" Frank started to say when Greg's Porsche roared into the driveway and left a strip of burning rubber. Greg, Mike, and Callie scrambled out of the car.

"What the—?" said Frank as he jumped out of the van.

"Callie, what are you doing here?" Joe asked, finishing the question.

"Some guy drove up behind us on a deserted street and tried to run us off the road," she said, breathless with excitement. "The first time the car came up beside us, Greg stepped on the gas, and you should have seen the Porsche accelerate—it went off like a rocket."

"I've done a little work on the engine," Greg said. "Nothing much, really, but it gives it a few more horses. It was pretty easy to get away."

"Don't be modest," Callie said. "You drove like an Indie Five Hundred winner. But what was really great was how you kept your head when he did catch up with us and smashed into our rear."

"Smashed your car?" said Joe.

"He just dented the fender some," said Greg.

"But whoever it was meant business. He tried to cut us off, but we got away."

"Thanks to the way you maneuvered the car," said Callie. "It was really cool. He almost went off the road himself once. And the way you took those turns to finally shake him. I wouldn't mind having you on hand to drive me anytime."

When Frank saw how she was looking at Greg, it was hard for him to turn his attention to the case.

"So somebody was out to get you," he said. "I wonder why." He turned to Callie. "I know you might not like this, but we can't go to the police. We're in the middle of a case, and it might put someone's life in danger."

"Greg already thought of that," Callie said as they headed for the house. "He told me all about it on the way here."

"Right, she's part of the team now," said Mike. "She said it wasn't the first time she'd gotten involved with one of your cases."

"Somehow she almost always manages to," said Joe with a sigh. Having Callie on a case bothered him. Since his girlfriend, Iola Morton, had been killed on one of their cases, Joe didn't like girls helping them. The fact that Callie had shown she was able to take care of herself time after time really didn't matter to him.

Frank decided to get the subject back on track. It was time to use his deductive powers, if only to remind Callie that solving a case demanded calm, cool brain work, not merely quick reflexes.

"I'm sure Callie can help us," he said, holding the door open for Joe and her. "But first, let's figure out why you two have become targets, since that guy certainly couldn't have been after Callie."

"Not *guy, guys*—I spotted two of them in the car," said Greg. "Maybe they're on my stepfather's payroll. He might not want to take the chance that Mom told us whatever she found out about him."

"That makes sense," said Callie, leading the way into the living room. "I see you think as fast as you drive."

Frank tried not to notice the look she gave Greg. "Look, just because a guy dents your car, I don't think we should assume—" Joe began, but before he could continue, the phone rang.

Greg walked into the hall to answer it. He listened, muttered something into the receiver, and hung up. Then he returned to the others.

"It was my stepfather," he told them. "He said the kidnappers have gotten in touch to tell him where to bring the cash. And he said they insisted that he bring Mike and me with him to the drop."

"But why?" Callie asked.

"The kidnappers claim they want to keep the

whole family in sight so we don't try to pull a fast one. But I have a different idea."

"I think I have the same idea," said Mike. "That our stepfather is luring us into a trap?"

"Yeah," said Greg grimly. "A death trap."

Chapter

6

THE THREE OF them were standing under an unlit streetlight on a deserted midnight street in a rundown part of New York City. They looked completely out of place: a well-dressed, middle-aged man and two teenagers in windbreakers and neatly pressed jeans.

They hoped they also looked like Walter Rawley and his stepsons, Greg and Mike.

That was their plan. It was a long shot, but the only shot they had. It had been Dunn's idea.

He had phoned the Rawleys' right after Walter Rawley had called about the ransom demand. Through the tap on the phones, Dunn had heard everything.

He had left for Bayport immediately and must have broken all the speed limits driving there. He had arrived at the Rawleys' a little over an hour after the calls. They had decided to meet there since Walter Rawley had said he wouldn't come home that night. He had to go into New York to gather the ransom money. Greg and Mike were to meet him in the city later when the ransom was to be delivered.

They all sat in the living room to discuss Dunn's plan. "I'd have bet that the kidnapping story was a phony," said Greg, shaking his head.

"It still might be," said Dunn carefully. "Your stepfather could be covering his tracks because any kidnapping investigation would cover everything." He paused a second. "Especially if the victim turns up dead."

Mike raised an eyebrow at his brother.

Frank, who caught the look exchanged by the brothers, nodded. "Sure, Mr. Rawley could have staged the ransom call and put it on tape. That way he'd have proof that his story was genuine."

At this Joe raised a hand, palm out. "Hey, Frank, nobody knows Rawley's the bad guy. He's always been our friend, remember. We have to keep an open mind."

"Right," said Frank. "But we also have to explore all the possibilities. We can't let our feelings blind us."

Dunn smiled at Frank. "It's good to be working with a pro. Now listen to my plan. If there are

45

any weaknesses, maybe you can spot them, even suggest something better.''

"Sure," said Frank, and he and the others listened to Dunn outline his scheme.

Dunn had already put part of it into operation. As soon as Rawley had called the boys, Dunn called Rawley at his office and, in approximately the same muffled voice that the kidnapper had used, told him that the ransom drop-off had been pushed back from midnight to two A.M., and hung up. Then, using his contacts, he had had Rawley's phone cut off in case the kidnappers tried to reach him again.

"That'll give us the time we need," said Dunn. "I'm about the same size as Rawley. Frank and Joe, you're about the same sizes as Greg and Mike. If we wear their clothes, at a distance we could pass for them."

"But what happens when the kidnappers do get close enough to finger us?" asked Frank.

"*This* happens," said Dunn, and pulled his .45 out of his briefcase. "I'll have it in here where the money's supposed to be. Rawley's a businessman and may even be on their side, so they'll never expect him to carry a gun. I should be able to get the drop on them. I hope the gun will loosen their tongues."

Frank bit his lip and thought a moment. "Of course, if it fails, we might be putting Mrs. Rawley's life in extra danger."

46

"Yeah, I know," said Dunn, his voice wavering for a second. "But that's something that Greg and Mike have to think about. They have to decide if it's worth the chance. One other thing to consider—they might have killed her already. It's up to you to call it, boys."

He paused as Greg and Mike sucked in their breath together. Their eyes met, and then they looked back at Dunn. They each nodded once, giving him the okay.

"Okay," Dunn said softly. "But we do have to face the facts. If she *is* still alive, I don't know if they'll release her under any circumstances. Kidnappers rarely do." He then turned to Frank and Joe. "I'd give you two guns too, but you don't have licenses. You understand how it is."

"Right," said Frank. "We're okay without them."

Joe slapped the heavy ring of keys in his jacket and, grinning, said, "We could always do our quick-draw routine again."

Dunn remembered how the boys had disarmed him and sheepishly returned Joe's grin.

Six hours later they were standing on the dark New York street: Joe clenching and unclenching his hands impatiently, and Frank pacing in a tight little circle.

"We've been waiting here ten minutes," Joe said. "Think they'll show up?"

47

"Don't panic," said Dunn. "We got here a few minutes early so we would see them approach. Frank, Joe, you look down the street to the right; I'll take the left."

Frank and Joe nodded and did as told. And that was why no one saw the trouble before it came.

Not from the right. Not from the left. But from behind them, out of a pitch-black alley.

Too late Frank and Joe heard the thud and wheeled around to see Dunn crumpling to the sidewalk while a man in a black jogging suit and full black ski mask stood over him with a baseball bat in his hand. Beside him were two other men in masks; both had drawn guns, both were leveled at the Hardys.

"Hands on top of your heads—now," said one of them, while the first man knelt down and checked Dunn.

"He'll be okay," he decided. "I thought for a second I might have hit him too hard." Then he pulled out a miniature walkie-talkie from his pocket and spoke into it. "Got the kids. Let's go."

Frank and Joe exchanged a quick glance, wondering if they should make a break for it.

One of the men said, "Don't even think about it. One false move, and you're dead. Keep your hands on your heads, your eyes straight ahead, and your mouths shut."

48

The other gunman added, "Don't worry about getting tired. You don't have long to wait."

He was telling the truth. Less than two minutes later a long black car came around the corner and pulled up beside them. The driver wore a black ski mask too.

"Now lower your hands and put them behind your backs—real slow," commanded the goon who had knocked out Dunn. At the same time the other two moved forward and pressed their guns against the Hardys' ears. First Frank, then Joe, felt cold metal handcuffs being snapped around their wrists.

"Get in the back," the man with the bat ordered.

The door slammed behind them, and one of the gunman got into the front seat beside the driver. He turned to keep his gun trained on the Hardys. "Okay, let's deliver Greg and Mike to headquarters," he ordered the driver.

The Hardys had the satisfaction of knowing that part of their plan had succeeded. The crooks believed they were the Rawleys. But Frank and Joe had to come up with a new plan now. A plan of escape.

All they could do for the moment, though, was keep a sharp lookout and be ready for any opening.

Through the window they could see the landscape, lit by the ghostly light of the moon. It looked as desolate as the moon's surface far from the glittering world of Broadway and theaters. Fields of rubble from demolished sites lay among the crumbling shells of abandoned and burnt-out buildings. The only way to save this neighborhood would be to plow it under and start over.

The car stopped in front of a building that appeared to be in decent shape—until the boys looked closely and saw that all the windows were made of cardboard painted to look like sparkling new glass protecting lovely new apartments. Frank remembered reading about buildings like this in the paper. City officials had not had the funds to make the buildings fit to live in, so they decided to spend what money they had to make the shells *look* inhabited. They claimed it would improve the image of the neighborhood. No one, though, had been fooled. Everyone knew the buildings were deserted.

Except this one.

Frank and Joe were herded out. Then the driver knocked three times, paused, and knocked three times again on a sheet-metal door while the gunman kept the Hardys covered. The door was opened by a tall muscle-bound man in jeans and a white T-shirt pulled taut across his pumped-up chest. They all entered, Frank and Joe went first, prodded along by the gun barrel.

Inside, dim electric lights showed that someone

had set up crude living quarters in a few of the rooms off the crumbling center hallway.

"Welcome to the Hilton, kids," the man in the T-shirt said with a big, gap-toothed grin. "We hope you enjoy your stay."

"Too bad it's going to be for such a short time," said the gunman, shaking his head slowly from side to side.

"Well, that's this part of town for you." The driver added his bit. "Not a nice place to visit—but such an easy place to die in."

Chapter

7

FRANK DECIDED TO start asking questions, to find out what was happening—and to postpone what seemed inevitable.

"Do you really think you're going to get the money?" he asked. "You snatch our mother, bash our stepfather till he's probably dead, and grab us. There's nobody left to pay you."

"I wouldn't worry about your stepfather," said the gap-toothed man. "He ain't dead. That was a love tap we gave him. You know, just enough to put a nice realistic bump on his head—so the cops would believe his story about being knocked out. And we already got our money."

Frank swallowed hard. So it was true. Mr. Rawley was tied up with the crooks.

But—then again, maybe he wasn't. Maybe the

guy was lying. That would be one way of concealing who was running this show.

Joe was shaking his head in disbelief. He had believed so strongly that Walter Rawley was innocent that nothing short of hard evidence would convince him of Rawley's guilt. Hard evidence was what they had to find. But first they had to figure out a way to stay alive long enough to look for it.

"You're trying to tell us that our stepfather is mixed up with you?" Frank said scornfully. "Who do you think you're talking to? We're young, but not dumb."

"Save your fairy tales for bedtime, bonzo." Joe added.

The man in the white T-shirt answered sarcastically. "Hey, *sorry*. I didn't realize I was dealing with such cool customers. Looks like I have to find somebody you will believe. Fortunately, I got the perfect person. Come on, wise guys."

He gestured to the gunman to follow with Frank and Joe. "This way. Down the hall," he commanded. .

Down the hall another gunman stood guard in front of a metal door.

"Open it up, Jack. We got two more guests."

Jack unlocked the door, and the first gunman said, "Okay, kiddies, in you go. And no funny business. I'd just as soon squeeze this trigger now as later. The only reason you're still alive is that I have my orders."

Frank was expecting to see her, and so was Joe. There was only one person who could be in that candlelit room.

Linda Rawley.

The chic red dress she was wearing hung in a mass of wrinkles. Her blond hair was disheveled, her makeup smudged. And there was terror in her blue eyes.

"Hey, lady, you got visitors," the gunman said from the doorway. "Your own darling little boys. Aren't you going to thank me for arranging this nice little family reunion?"

Linda Rawley's mouth literally dropped open when she saw Frank and Joe. It took her a moment to find her voice, and when she did, it was high and pinched. "What is this? Some kind of a joke?"

"No joke," the gunman assured her. "You told us how close you are to your sons, so we figured you'd want to be with them."

By now Linda Rawley had gotten control of herself. Her voice was strong as she said, "What are you talking about? These aren't my sons. They're Frank and Joe Hardy, two kids my sons know."

"What the—" Gap-Tooth said. Then he paused, and his voice filled with contempt. "You

54

aren't fooling me, lady. You're playing out of your league trying to outfox us.''

"And I tell you these aren't my boys—thank God," said Linda Rawley defiantly. "You people have fouled up." She turned to the Hardys. "Frank, Joe, do you have anything that might convince these idiots?"

"But—" Frank started to say.

"Believe me, I know what I'm doing," Linda Rawley pleaded softly. "I'll explain later. But right now, do what I say, *please*. Show these men who you really are."

There was no arguing with the desperation in her voice, in her eyes.

"Okay if we reach in our back pockets for our wallets?" Frank asked.

The man shrugged. "Okay, but do it slow. Remember, there are two guns on you."

Frank and Joe were careful to obey orders. Then, while Jack held his gun on them, the first gunman and the muscle-bound guy went through the wallets, examining the Hardys' driver's licenses and other ID.

"Look real—but I have to check it out," the man said. "Meanwhile, you can keep breathing until the boss tells me how, when, and where you stop."

He turned to Jack and said, "I'm giving the boss a call. Lock up, and stay awake guarding the door. We can't afford a slip-up."

"Hey, what about our wallets?" Joe demanded.

"What about that, I almost forgot to give them back," he said sarcastically. "But maybe I ought to hold on to them for safekeeping. You're in a real bad neighborhood, you know. Full of people who'd slit your throat for a buck." He grinned at his own joke, then added, "While you're at it, you kids better empty out your pockets and toss me what's in them. I wouldn't want you having anything that could get you into trouble."

The Hardys had no choice but to obey. The men looked over the coins and keys they tossed out. The gorilla held up a prize to the flickering candlelight. "A Swiss army knife. That's a baddie. A toy like this could give you kids all kind of dangerous ideas."

Pocketing the loot, he walked out of the room, followed by the other two. The door was slammed and the metal vibrated like distant thunder. Finally a bolt was thrown with a loud click.

Joe stared at the door. "A month's allowance," he said mournfully.

"Forget it. There's nothing you can buy in here," said Frank. He turned to Linda Rawley, waiting for an explanation.

"If they thought you were really Greg and Mike, we'd all be dead within the hour."

"Why? What do you mean?" asked Joe.

"That's complicated," Mrs. Rawley said. She

motioned for them to join her by the room's only window, which was covered over with one piece of sheet metal. She said to them in a low voice, "I don't want anyone listening from the other side of the door."

"Good," Frank whispered back. "But we've got to be even more careful."

Each took one side of the room and checked the floors, walls, and ceiling for any sign of an electronic bug.

When they were finished, Frank said, "Looks like the room is clean. I think it's safe to talk as long as we whisper."

"Then I'll begin at the beginning of this nightmare," said Linda Rawley. "Walter and I decided to remodel the bedroom—enlarge the closets, repaper, things like that." She stared off for a moment, as if she was seeing another, happier time. "When the workmen were ripping out what had been Joanne's—Walter's first wife's—closet, they found this little red book in an envelope at the back of a shelf in a corner of the closet. The book turned out to be Joanne's diary."

"It must have been there for a long time," said Frank. "She died in that car accident years ago."

"The first entry was made a year before she died. Anyway, it's hard to resist reading a diary. I couldn't, at least. The first entries weren't very interesting, and I was about to stop reading. Then she began to write about Walter's recent activities. He was staying out late, making secretive phone calls, leaving the house at all hours. The first thing she suspected was another woman. But it wasn't that. It was worse." Linda Rawley paused and looked down at her hands. "A lot worse."

Frank and Joe glanced at each other. What had he been into? Drugs? Gambling? Embezzlement?

"Piece by piece Joanne Rawley put together the puzzle," Linda Rawley said. "It looked like Walter was involved with foreign intelligence agents. They had given him the money to start his electronics firm, and as the company got more and more top government contracts, he was repaying them with super-classified technical information."

"Did Joanne report this to the authorities?" asked Frank, thinking it couldn't be true that Walter Rawley was a spy.

"She was going to—when she was absolutely sure of what she suspected," Linda Rawley said. "But she hadn't enough hard evidence to confirm her suspicions, and she loved her husband too much to accuse him without positive proof that he was guilty." Linda Rawley swallowed hard. "She never did get the evidence she was looking for. The diary ended abruptly—with one last terrifying entry . . ." Her voice trailed off.

"What was it?" asked Frank gently.

Mrs. Rawley took one deep breath and began.

"Joanne had a habit of tying a thin, almost invisible thread around the metal catch of her diary, to make sure that no one found it in her drawer and read it. In her last entry she wrote that the thread had been snapped, and that she was afraid, horribly afraid, that someone had read it. She was even more afraid of who that someone was. Her husband—Walter. That was why she hid the diary—in case something happened to her." Linda Rawley shook her head, and her voice was as chill as death. "That last entry was dated the day of Joanne's car accident—the accident that ended her life."

"And you think—?" asked Joe. He didn't have to finish the sentence. What else was there to think?

Frank finally broke the silence. He tried to get the conversation back to the dangers of the present. "So what did you do when you read the diary?"

"Nothing." Linda Rawley sighed. "You see, I loved Walter too. So I decided to wait until I was sure, one way or another. I'm sure now, but now it's too late."

"I'm still confused, Mrs. Rawley," Frank said. "Who do you think did this to you?"

"I—I don't see any other explanation," Linda Rawley stammered. "The only person who could have had me kidnapped was my husband. I knew I was in trouble when he came home unexpectedly and found me rereading Joanne's diary. I shoved it into my purse quickly and tried to tell myself that he hadn't noticed. He said nothing about it. I know now how foolish that was of me. I found out when those men kidnapped me. The first thing they showed me was the diary that someone had stolen from my safe. All they wanted to know was if I told anyone what I found. They promised to hurt me unless I told them." Linda shuddered. "It was then that I came up with the lie that saved my life—for the time being, anyway."

"And that was?" asked Joe.

"I think I know already," said Frank. "You told them that you had let Greg and Mike in on the secret. That's why you didn't want them to think we were your sons. Otherwise they would have killed us all. But with Greg and Mike still free, they can use us to force Greg and Mike to keep quiet.

Linda Rawley nodded. "You've figured out everything. Everything, except that I didn't tell them that my sons had the information. I told them that I had made a photocopy of the diary. Greg and Mike were to pick up the copy if they found out I met with any kind of fatal accident."

"You're pretty fast when you need to be," Frank commented.

"It's amazing how fast you can think when you're facing death," Linda Rawley observed.

"I hope you're right," said Joe, looking around the room for a way to escape. "Because it'll be really amazing if we get out of this place alive."

Chapter

8

LINDA RAWLEY SHOOK her head in despair. "I haven't been able to think of a way out of here," she said softly. "We're caged in. Four solid walls—the only window sealed—and a guard right outside the only door. I feel like a rat in a trap."

"Except that it's the rats who have us in a trap," said Frank, his eyes slowly taking in all the walls—all four corners.

The room was bare except for the solitary candle standing vigil in the center.

"I've been here for over twenty-four hours—and I'm being driven slowly mad," Linda Rawley groaned. In frustration she slammed the palm of her hand against the sheet-metal covering the window. The sound bounced off the four walls and echoed faster and faster for a couple of seconds until it stopped.

Suddenly Frank was alert. "Hey, do that again," he said, excitement in his voice. "No, on second thought, don't. I'll do it. Mrs. Rawley, can I borrow your scarf?"

"Of course," she said, picking up the light silk scarf that had been lying on the floor and handing it to Frank.

"It'll muffle the noise," he explained, wrapping it around his hand. Making a fist, he hit the sheet metal close to one side of the window. No reverberation that way.

"That's what I thought," he said, peering at it closely. "Look, it's coming loose. Now if we just had something to dig the nails out."

"As a matter of fact, we do," said Joe. With the flourish of a magician pulling a rabbit from a hat, he pulled his Swiss army knife from his pocket.

Frank's face lit up in an appreciative smile. "Nice job of palming it."

"Nothing that any other brilliant, resourceful, and talented guy couldn't do," said Joe, prying the metal up. "The nails are coming away nice and easy."

"It's an old building and the wood frame must be rotten," said Frank.

Joe hummed the tune "I Love New York" as he gave the sheet metal one hard tug. He quickly

63

laid his palm against the center to deaden the vibrations. It swung far enough away from the window to leave them the space they needed to exit.

"Good thing we're on the ground floor. Ladies first," Joe said, instinctively stepping aside to let Linda Rawley out. Then he reconsidered. "I'd better lead the way to see if these rats have guards outside."

He boosted himself up and over the window ledge and dropped soundlessly onto the concrete alley. "The coast is clear. Come on out. It's a beautiful night," he whispered back in.

It was a beautiful night, Frank thought. If you craned your neck to look up at the slit of starlit sky high above the dank alley that the window opened onto.

But the three of them didn't stand still long enough to stargaze or take in the garbage-scented air.

They started moving soundlessly toward the the end of the alleyway, and when they reached it they looked back to the left and saw something that made them sprint silently off in the opposite direction.

Someone was guarding the front of the building. They didn't wait to see who. Just as they thought they had gotten away clean, Frank stumbled into a hubcap lying buried under a newspaper.

Behind them the man shouted. Suddenly bullets were whizzing near them, chipping showers of brick off buildings and ricocheting off wheelless abandoned cars. The man had a silenced automatic weapon. As he ran Frank wondered why he bothered with a silencer. There was no one to hear the gunfire in this neighborhood.

They tore around a corner, praying that the gunman would be as slow in chasing them as he was bad at shooting them.

Suddenly a pair of headlights caught them in a white shaft of light, blinding them like deer on a highway.

They came to a stumbling halt, almost tripping over one another as the car skidded to a stop not three feet from them.

They all held their breath, forgetting to exhale. To have escaped and then to be captured so quickly seemed so unfair.

"Hop in. Quick."

It was Greg! With him in the front seat of a car they couldn't identify was Mike. And holding the back door open was Callie.

No time for questions. Joe shoved Mrs. Rawley into the backseat before he and Frank dove in and pulled the door shut. The car shot into motion, made a screeching U-turn, and headed out of the neighborhood through deserted streets.

It was only when they were back in midtown Manhattan and Greg had parked the car that they had a chance to get out and talk. First the boys hugged and spoke with their mother.

Then Frank asked, "How did you find us?"

Greg grinned. "You're not the only one who can do detective work."

Callie seconded him. "He's right about that. I saw him in action. He's good—really good. You ought to think about making him part of your team."

Despite himself, Frank started to glower. But he stopped and told himself not to be dumb. "Yeah, good work. But how did you pull it off? What did you do?"

"Wasn't hard, really," said Greg with a brief show of modesty. "After you guys and Dunn cut out for the rendezvous, Mike and I figured you might need some backup. So we went by Walter's office to tell him we'd meet him just before the drop. Then we arrived at the delivery spot just in time to watch Dunn get slugged and you get grabbed. By the time we ran back to our car you'd vanished. So we figured the best thing we could do was cruise the streets, hoping to spot a car parked somewhere."

"And what's Callie doing with you?" asked Frank.

Callie answered for herself. "Just before Greg and Mike left, 'Callie' gave them a call to see how things were going. Greg told me their plan, and I asked if I could come."

"And I said sure," Greg chimed in. "I figured we needed all the help we could get and Callie can really handle herself."

Callie flashed a triumphant look at Joe. "Thanks, Greg, I appreciate that," she said, her voice warm.

Frank didn't feel warm. He felt hot—under the collar. Fortunately, Callie was standing where she couldn't see how angry he was becoming. But Joe could.

"Looks like you don't have to join our team," Joe said, speaking to Callie. "Looks like you and Greg can form a team of your own."

"Time to cut the small talk," said Frank sharply. "We have to figure out our next move. Like finding Dunn, for instance."

"Dunn's okay," Mike said. "We checked him out after the guys who grabbed you lost us. He would have helped us look for you, but he wanted to check out a couple of other leads."

Greg glanced at his watch. "Mike and I have to join Walter now, to go through with that charade with the ransom. I can hardly wait to see his face when *we* show up and nobody comes to snatch Mike and me."

"But do you think it'll be safe for you?" asked Callie. "If your stepfather is involved in this kidnapping, won't someone have told him what's happened?"

"Doesn't matter if he has been clued in or

not," Greg said. "Even if he has been, he knows Mom's free now, so there's no point in grabbing Mike and me, especially since Mom knows where the hideout is and can tip off the cops. All he'll want to do now is cover his tracks—until he can get away."

"Seems like you've thought of everything," said Callie.

"Still, you may not have covered all the angles," Frank said, cutting in. "To be on the safe side, Joe and I will play backup for you two. Turnabout's fair play."

"Okay, if you want to," said Greg. "But it's not really necessary. Dunn should be able to do it. He'll be checking his answering machine every ten minutes so we can get in touch with him whenever we need to."

"I figure he won't mind some help," said Joe. "I'd like to get my hands on those guys who snatched us."

"I'll be on the backup team too," said Callie, looking at Joe to see if he dared voice an objection. Seeing the defiant look in her eyes, he kept his mouth shut.

"And I'll go too," Linda Rawley said simply. "I might not be able to help much, but I am your mother, and I couldn't stand the torture of waiting and worrying that something might have gone wrong."

"Come on, Mom, nothing'll go wrong, and

we'd feel better if we knew you were safe," said Greg.

"Yeah. It really would be better if you were out of sight," Mike added. "We should find a hiding place for you until we figure out how and what to tell the cops."

"Right," Greg said "We still can't go to them because we don't have enough evidence to put together a really convincing case against Walter."

Frank hated to say, "I agree," but he did. "The police do have to have evidence and follow procedures, and all that takes time that we don't have."

"Fast thinking and fast moving are the name of the game now," Joe added.

"Well, the name of *my* game is motherhood," said Linda Rawley firmly. "I'm going along."

They all recognized that tone of her voice. And there was no arguing with it.

Half an hour later Linda Rawley was with Frank, Joe, Callie, and Dunn as they crouched in an alley, waiting for Walter Rawley and his stepsons to arrive at the drop.

"I pray that everything will go all right," she said, her voice trembling.

"No reason it shouldn't." Frank tried to reassure her. "The kidnappers either won't bother to show up, or if they do show up, it'll just be to take the money and run, to convince Greg and Mike that the kidnapping was on the up-and-up.''

"I hope you're right," said Linda Rawley, unconvinced.

"We are," said Joe confidently. "Frank and I have had experience with this kind of thing."

"Quiet!" Dunn commanded in a harsh whisper. "Here they come."

Walter Rawley's gleaming Mercedes, looking as out of place in that neighborhood as a fish on a bicycle, pulled up to the curb and stopped. Walter, Greg, and Mike got out and stood under the same burnt-out streetlight. In the faint glow from streetlights farther down the street, the five people spying from the alley could see that Rawley was carrying a briefcase.

This time no goons sneaked out of the alley to jump them. But in a couple of minutes a black sedan did inch slowly down the street and pulled up just in front of the Mercedes.

Rawley and his stepsons turned toward the black car expectantly.

But nobody *expected* what came next.

Two men with handguns jumped out of the black car. They tore the briefcase out of Walter Rawley's hand and hustled Greg and Mike at gunpoint into the backseat of the car. Walter Rawley stood empty-handed and openmouthed as the car roared off.

In the alley the five onlookers stood open-mouthed too.

Linda Rawley found her voice first.

"You were all wrong," she whispered. "Dead wrong!"

Chapter

9

"WHY AREN'T WE chasing them?" Callie asked.

"They're long gone," said Dunn. "It'll be better to keep an eye on Walter, to see what he does now."

Walter Rawley stood still, shaking his head back and forth like a man trying to clear his brain after taking a bad punch.

"Looks like he really is stunned," said Frank. "Maybe he isn't in on the kidnapping."

"Looks can be deceiving," said Dunn. "Let's see what he does now."

Walter Rawley had regained his balance and frantically looked around. Finally he ran for his car and roared away, leaving only exhaust behind him.

"Well, it looked like he was making sure no

one was watching him," Dunn said, stepping out of the alley.

"You don't trust anybody," commented Joe. "He was looking for help. He'd just been mugged. He panicked, he doesn't know what to do. He's lost his whole family."

"Well, I've lost my sons, and I don't understand why," Linda Rawley said, interrupting.

"To buy time," Frank explained to her.

"Time to hunt you down," Dunn added bluntly. "And get rid of you. And not only you. You two as well, Frank and Joe. If they're as good as they seem to be, and if Walter Rawley is their boss, they have to silence all witnesses."

By now Callie could restrain herself no longer. Impatiently she said, "While you guys are trading theories, the kidnappers and Rawley are getting away."

"It all happened too fast. We didn't really think anyone would have showed up," Joe said calmly. "There's no way we could follow."

"We don't have any more time to waste now. I say we should call the police—and do it now," Callie insisted.

"No. You can't," Linda Rawley cried. "My boys—they'd be killed!"

"I'm afraid she's right, Callie," Frank said. "That's why they snatched Greg and Mike. They know she won't dare go to the police while they have her sons."

"But we've got to do *something*," Callie insisted.

"We need facts," said Frank. "If we get enough evidence to finger Rawley, he wouldn't dare have his men hurt Greg and Mike. Even if it's not Rawley, we need the facts to track them down."

"Tell me, Linda," said Dunn, "is there someone in your husband's business, someone who works closely with him, who might know about anything irregular that's happening with the business?"

She thought a moment. "I'm not sure. He never really talks to me about his work. But I do know he has a private secretary who's been with him a long time. A man named William Clark. I've met him a few times. A mousy little man."

"That's a start," said Dunn. "Where does he live?"

"In Bayport," Linda Rawley said.

"Frank, Joe, see what you can find out from him," Dunn said. "I'll check out the place where the kidnappers held you, but I know it's a waste of time. Still I have to check out everything. Then I'll go to the city to nose around and get a lead on the kidnappers."

"We still have to figure out a way to shield Mrs. Rawley until we put the kidnappers out of business," Joe said.

"I've got the perfect answer," said Callie.

Blood Relations

"They have no idea I'm involved in this. Why doesn't Mrs. Rawley stay at my house? My parents are off on a week's vacation, so I'm there alone."

"Great idea," said Frank. "It won't take us that long to track down the kidnappers and get Greg and Mike back."

"And get the goods on Walter Rawley," added Dunn.

"No matter how much evidence you find against him," Mrs. Rawley blurted out, her voice thick with sadness, "I'll find it impossible to believe."

"I understand, Linda," said Dunn sympathetically. "And I'm sorry. I feel we should get going now. Will you be all right?"

She drew a deep breath and nodded.

"You know, it really bugs me," Joe said to Frank after they had dropped Linda Rawley and Callie off at Callie's house. "Everyone but me seems to have convicted Mr. Rawley already. I always thought a man was considered innocent until proven guilty."

"That's a new line from you, Joe," said Frank, raising an eyebrow at him. "Usually you're the one who's eager to act first and ask questions later."

"Maybe it's because this is all too easy—all too pat," Joe said. "Seems like we're missing something because we're so eager to nail Rawley. And I think *somebody* has to keep that in mind just to be fair.''

Frank frowned as he steered the van toward their house. ''You think I like accusing an old family friend?'' he demanded of Joe. ''I don't like it any more than you do.''

''We have to be sure,'' Joe insisted.

''Yeah, I agree. We need facts. But we've gone after people with a lot less evidence than this before.''

The brothers rode in silence for a minute. ''Maybe we've been wrong,'' Frank finally said. ''Maybe we should bring Dad in on this.''

''No way.'' Joe shook his head. ''Dad would feel like he had to talk to Mr. Rawley himself, and if he is innocent, it would ruin their friendship and maybe even Rawley's reputation. If he is guilty he'd be tipped off that we were on to him, and he could clear out.''

''I don't know, brother,'' Frank said, turning the van into the Hardys' driveway. ''All I know is, we've gotten ourselves into a real mess this time.''

''Yeah, but at least we're home in time to catch a couple of hours' sleep before we talk to Clark.''

Frank and Joe slept in their clothes and got up just as their parents were sitting down to the morning meal.

Their mother, Laura Hardy, merely lifted her eyebrows quizzically when they strolled into the kitchen. Then she smiled and set two more places at the table.

The only reference she made to their outfits was, "You two planning on wearing those clothes for the rest of your lives?"

Their father, Fenton Hardy, added, "I see your vacation from work has ended. Hope things are going okay."

In most matters Fenton Hardy's relationship with Frank and Joe was that of a father, both in giving them advice and laying down ground rules. But where their detective work was concerned, he treated them as equals, merely offering help when asked and staying out of their way the rest of the time.

"Everything's going fine," Joe said. "A routine investigation. Confidential, of course, but pretty cut and dried. We should wrap it up quick."

"Any possibility of our getting any breakfast?" Frank asked.

"Pancakes coming up," said Laura Hardy. "But I hope you great detectives will use your powers of observation afterward. There will be dirty dishes and pans in the sink. Please observe them and deduce that I'll be late for my work at the planning commission if I wash them."

After breakfast Fenton Hardy helped his sons

with the cleaning up, then headed for his study in another part of the house.

Joe, stacking the last of the dishes in the washer, turned to Frank and said, "It's funny. I thought I'd still be sleepy, but I'm not the least bit tired."

"You know, now that you mention it, I'm not either," said Frank.

"Matter of fact, I feel raring to go," said Joe.

By now, neither of them could hold back their grins. It felt good to be going into action again on their own. Teaming up with others was okay, to a point. But they liked it a whole lot better when they were working their own way.

"What do you think, Joe, white collar or black bag?"

"I think this is a white-collar job," said Joe.

A "black bag" job involved lying low and eavesdropping. A "white collar" job was one in which the boys put on their best-looking suits and adopted a slightly officious manner and never stopped talking.

Joe once told a friend that "when they open the door to us in our three-piece suits, we've got it made. We don't let them get rid of us even if all they say is 'go away.' "

The boys had tried every kind of disguise and found that the most important part of any costume was their attitude. It was all a matter of staying in character. If they acted as if they were

78

supposed to be asking questions, most people just answered them.

An hour later two very different young men emerged from the Hardy house. Showered and very conservatively dressed in suits and ties, Joe and Frank were, at least for the moment, two young investigators from the Internal Revenue Service.

They parked a block from Clark's house, well out of sight. Joe's van was not suitable transportation for any agent of the IRS, no matter how young he and his partner were.

Clark wasn't hard to find. His address was listed. The house was a nondescript clapboard bungalow in a respectable but slightly shabby neighborhood, the kind where lawns are nicely trimmed and the windows are clean but most of the houses could use a fresh coat of paint.

"Guess Mr. Rawley doesn't pay his secretary too well," said Joe.

"Maybe Clark likes to save his money," said Frank. "Or maybe this house is a cover and Clark figures, if you've got it, *don't* flaunt it."

Frank pressed the door buzzer. They could hear it sound inside. But there was no answer.

"No luck," said Frank, disappointed. "Nobody's home." But before he turned away, he tried the doorknob automatically, just to do *something*.

To his surprise, the door swung open.

He turned to Joe.

"Should we?" he asked.

"Why not?" said Joe, already on his way in.

"You never know what you can find," agreed Frank, following at his heels.

"You're not kidding," Joe gasped. *"Look!"*

But Frank already was looking—at the body lying dead on the floor.

He didn't have time to look at it long.

"Up with your hands," a voice growled.

And Frank and Joe wheeled around to find themselves looking down the barrel of a .45.

Chapter

10

THE MAN WITH the gun instantly recognized them.

"Well, well, look who's here," he said with a nasty grin. "What a surprise."

They recognized him too. The gunman who had kidnapped them and herded them into the abandoned building.

"Yeah, we're getting to be old friends," Joe wisecracked. "And we haven't even been introduced."

"You can call me Max," the man said. "And I got your names already. Frank and Joe Hardy, right?"

"What makes you so sure this time?" asked Frank.

"Let's say we have a mutual friend," Max said.

THE HARDY BOYS CASEFILES

Then his eyes lit up as a thought hit him. "In fact, we got two mutual friends." The gunman indicated the body on the floor. "I didn't know you were pals with this Clark character. But that's fine with me. You can help me find what I was looking for when you barged in."

"What's that?" Frank asked, sizing up the situation and trying to spot a way out of their jam. But Max was alert as well, the gun steady in his hand. The guy was a pro.

"The company books," Max said. "There's a copy of Rawley's company's records here somewhere. Clark wouldn't tell me where they were and you see what happened to him. I advise you to tell me while you still got breath to do it with."

"We don't know anything about that, honest," Frank protested.

"Then what are you doing here—selling Girl Scout cookies?" Max asked. "Talk, or I'll lay you down next to this piece of meat."

"Look, you're making a mistake," said Joe, trying to sound convincing.

"You're making the mistake," Max said. "The last one you'll ever make."

"Joe's telling the truth," said Frank, trying one last time to persuade the gunman. "We don't know anything about these records, but we'll help you search for them. That's right up our alley. We're experienced investigators."

"What kind of jerk do you think I am?" Max

82

said scornfully. "You'd jump me the first time I took my eyes off you. Well, I'm not giving you the chance. I'll find the stuff alone, without either of you getting in my way."

He pointed the gun so it was aimed directly between Joe's eyes.

"Bye-bye, Joey," he said. "Your brother Frank will be along in a minute."

With an effort, Joe kept his eyes open. There had to be a way out of this. There had to be. No way it could end like this, so fast.

"Bye-bye," Max said, and Joe tensed, cold sweat on his skin.

Sound exploded. But it wasn't the bang of a gun. It was glass shattering.

A rock had come through the hall window and knocked Max's gun aside.

"Drop it," a voice commanded.

Max didn't obey. But he didn't shoot Joe either. He had a better use for his time. He wheeled around and ran for the back door.

Frank and Joe took off after him at breakneck speed. As he rounded the corner into the kitchen, Joe caught his foot in a scatter rug and down he went. Frank tripped over him and sprawled spread-eagle on top of Joe.

"He got away!" Frank said, scrambling to his feet.

All they could do now was wonder who had saved them. They rushed back into the front hall.

A moment later Greg and Mike charged in through the front door.

"Whew, that was close," Greg said. "We watched through the window for as long as possible. We were hoping you'd disarm him so we wouldn't have to risk your lives by trying something."

"But when he was about to shoot, we had to gamble on him panicking," said Mike.

"It was a good gamble," said Frank. "He's not crazy: he's a pro. And a pro's first rule is to survive."

Joe shook his head, astounded by his brother. It was just like Frank to start in analyzing events rather than asking the obvious first question. Joe did it. "How did you guys get away from the kidnappers?"

"We had a little luck," Greg said.

"Greg's being modest," Mike said. "Luck didn't have anything to do with it. Greg waited till there was just one guard, then he faked the guy out by pretending to have a stomachache. When the guard came to check, Greg got the drop on him, and we got out of the apartment they were holding us in. Callie said it sounded like Greg had been taking superhero pills."

Greg smiled modestly while his brother recounted their adventure.

Smiling was the last thing Frank felt like doing. He had a hard time keeping the sharpness out of his voice when he asked, "Callie? How did Callie find out?"

"As soon as we were free, we contacted Dunn," Greg explained. "He told us Mom was hiding out at Callie's, and we headed right over there. When we arrived, they told us what had happened."

"Then Mom told us you were going to pay a call on this William Clark guy," Mike said, continuing the story. "When we were being held prisoner, we heard them mention him a couple of times. We tried to call you, but you'd already left, so we rushed over here to see if you needed help. Guess it was a good thing we did."

"Sure was," Joe said.

"Look," Frank said impatiently, "we have more important things to worry about. Starting with the late Mr. Clark. Now we do have to call the police, but before we do, let's see if we can find those financial records Max talked about."

"Shouldn't we let the cops do that?" suggested Joe.

"I'd rather pursue this on our own a little further," Frank said. "If Mr. Rawley is a spy, and discovers the police are after him, he'll head for the border. I don't want to risk that. I think it's better that we get all the goods on him first, so that when the police come, it'll be with handcuffs."

"I'm glad you have a good reason," said Joe,

teasing. "I'd hate to think you were just trying to outdo old Greg here."

"This is a case, not a competition!" Frank said indignantly. "Why would I want to do that?"

"No reason," Joe grinned. "No reason at all."

"Come on, guys," Greg said. "Let's get going and see who can find the records first."

"That's the wrong way to look at it," Frank said. "We have to work together. And be sure not to leave fingerprints everywhere. The police *are* going to be all over this place."

But despite what he said, he felt himself moving into action like a sprinter off the starting line. The others were moving too, fanning out through the house.

Less than ten minutes later, Frank's voice rang out through the bungalow. "I found it!"

His voice came from the kitchen. Joe, Greg, and Mike joined him there. He was standing with a small microfilm canister in his hand. The canister was covered with flour, so were his hands. An open tin of flour was on the counter in front of him.

"It wasn't hard to find," Frank said. "This William Clark was a real tidy guy. You know that by the way he kept this house. The whole place is immaculate, as though he vacuumed it every day. But I spotted a trace of flour on the kitchen counter. He must have been in a hurry when he stuck the microfilm in the flour tin, and didn't have a chance to clean up afterward, or maybe he simply had too much on his mind."

"Outstanding," said Greg. "I couldn't have done better myself."

Frank found himself gritting his teeth. But he kept his cool. "No problem. When somebody's real scared, he tends to act out of character. I had a hunch that Clark was scared, and I kept my eyes open."

"Still, great work," Mike said. "Let's get out of here."

"Mike, you clean up the flour and I'll call the police," said Greg. "I'll make it an anonymous phone call. I'll tell them there's a corpse here, describe the gunman, and hang up. That way they'll be able to pursue their investigation while we're free to keep on with ours. Sound okay to you?"

"Good thinking," Frank admitted, putting the microfilm in his pocket. Joe wet a sponge and started removing all traces of the flour.

A minute later the clean-up was finished, but Greg returned shaking his head. "Wouldn't you know it," he said. "The line was busy. I'll give it five minutes and try again."

But that very minute, the phone rang.

"I'm going to answer it," Frank said. "I might be able to find out something about Clark; I'll tell whoever's calling that Clark is out and that he told me to take any messages that might come for him."

"Outstanding," said Greg, nodding. For some reason Greg was getting on Frank's nerves more and more.

But he tried to forget all about him when he answered the phone.

It was Linda Rawley, and it wasn't Clark she wanted.

"Thank goodness, Frank," she said. "I'm so worried. Callie went out to shop for food. She said she'd be right back, but that was almost an hour ago. Now I'm afraid something has happened."

"Sit tight," Frank answered, his voice tense. "We'll be over as soon as we take care of a couple of things here."

"Hurry," Linda Rawley pleaded.

"We will," Frank replied, and hung up. He kept his hand on the receiver. He was ready to pick up the phone and try the police again, hoping the line was clear by now.

Then the phone rang again.

He picked it up, but he didn't even have a chance to say hello before a gravelly voice said, "We've got Callie Shaw. You tell the cops about Clark or anything else, and they're going to have to work double time. Because your sweet little Callie'll be dead too!"

88

Chapter

11

"WHAT I CAN'T figure out is how they knew that Callie was working with us," Joe said. "Even Rawley didn't know, so we can't blame this on him." Joe and the others were having a conference in Callie's living room, trying to plan their next move. Frank was there, along with Greg and Mike and Linda Rawley. John Dunn had just arrived. He'd left New York as soon as they told him about Callie's kidnapping.

"Maybe they let Greg and Mike escape on purpose in order to tail them to their mother," Dunn speculated. "It would have been too dangerous, too risky to grab Linda here. The neighbors might have seen something suspicious. So they waited and grabbed Callie when she went to the store."

"I hate to admit it, but you might be right," said Greg ruefully. "We were so eager to make sure Mom was okay that we didn't look to see if we were being tailed."

"But how could they have tied Callie to Frank and me?" Joe wanted to know. "I mean, they called us at Clark's house with the news of the kidnapping."

"Our stepfather would have known that Callie and Frank were dating," Mike suggested. "Just like he would have known it was you two who were doing the snooping at Clark's."

"Still think the wonderful Walter Rawley is such a good guy, Joe?" Greg asked.

"Okay, okay," Joe said with a shrug of defeat. "Maybe I am wrong about him. Everybody's entitled to one mistake."

"Don't feel bad." Linda Rawley tried to comfort him. "I made an even bigger one. I married him, and he completely fooled me."

It was Frank who brought the group back to the problem at hand. "We're still stuck. Even with this new evidence, we can't go to the police. It would put Callie in too much danger."

"That's right," said Joe. "We have to find these guys by ourselves."

"What evidence do we have?" asked Dunn. He pointed at the microfilm canister on the coffee table in front of them. "Anybody check it out yet?"

"I gave it a quick once-over," said Frank. "It's a record of a lot of checks in large amounts over the years. They're from some company called Intertool, with an address in Lichtenstein and a checking account in an off-shore bank in the Bahamas."

"And who are they written to?" asked Greg. "Or can I guess?"

"I'm sure you can," acknowledged Frank.

"My dear stepfather, right?" Greg said, his mouth curling into a bitter sneer.

"It's still so hard for me to believe," Linda Rawley said.

"We have to face the facts," said Frank.

"Anything else on that microfilm?" asked Joe.

"A number—and the name and address of a bank in Zurich," said Frank.

"A numbered Swiss account," said Dunn, nodding. "It figures. It's the logical place for Rawley to squirrel away his dough."

"On our ski vacation in Switzerland last year, Walter did go off for a day to Zurich," Linda Rawley said, remembering. "He said it was business."

"Yeah. Funny business," commented Greg. "We've got the noose around stepdaddy's neck now."

"The question is, how do we pull it tight—without breaking an innocent neck," Frank said.

They sat silently thinking. But before any of

them could come up with an answer, the phone started ringing.

"I'll get it," said Frank. "It could be Callie's parents. They're used to me waiting around the house for Callie, so they won't be suspicious."

"Callie was right. You do cover all the angles," said Linda Rawley as Frank reached for the phone.

"She really say that?" said Frank, ignoring the ringing for a second.

"She really admires you," Linda Rawley assured him. "She talked about nothing but you while we were here."

Beaming, Frank picked up the phone and said hello. But his face fell instantly when he heard who was on the other end. He identified himself to the caller, then silently listened for a long time. Finally he said in a clipped voice, "Yeah, I hear you," and hung up.

He didn't have to tell the others who had called. They knew from the look on his face.

"The kidnappers want the microfilm fast—or else we get Callie back fast, in a box," he announced grimly. "They also say we shouldn't even think of making a copy of the film, since they're going to be watching us all the time. Personally, I think they're bluffing about that—but I'm not sure enough to risk Callie's life." He paused to see if the others agreed. They nodded. Then he added, "One more thing. They said they don't care what we tell the police about Clark. Seems they've done a real thorough housecleaning job. There's not a trace of the crime left—no corpse, not even a fingerprint."

"They don't miss a trick," said Dunn, shaking his head.

"So what," Joe said with a hint of anger in his voice. "Frank and I are pros. And we've been up against some of the best. These guys will make a mistake somewhere along the line. And when they do, we'll jump on it with both feet."

Frank, thinking of Callie, said, "I hope you're right."

So do I, Joe thought silently. But out loud he said, "Like I keep telling you, Frank, you've got to have faith."

At two A.M. Joe was still waiting for the kidnappers to make their first mistake.

He was standing hidden behind a stairway at one end of the platform inside a deserted subway station in the farthest reaches of Brooklyn.

At the other end of the platform Frank was hiding beneath an identical stairway.

Dunn was at the center of the platform with a briefcase containing the microfilm canister.

Their orders had been simple. Frank was supposed to show up with the microfilm and stand in the center of the platform. There the exchange would take place: the microfilm would be traded for Callie. After that, they were to forget all that had happened. This was to assure Callie's future safety. There would be no evidence to convince the police to pursue the matter. The Lichtenstein corporation, the Bahamas checking account, and the numbered Swiss savings account had all ceased to exist already.

Hearing the plan, Dunn had said, "That means we have to catch these people now. They're already dismantling the operation. Once they do, it'll be impossible to pin anything on them that'll stick."

Frank nodded. "We have to get our hands on at least one of them. But we have to make sure we get Callie safely out of it first. Otherwise, she's dead. With a murder rap for his first wife hanging over his head, Rawley won't have anything to lose by ordering another."

Dunn thought a moment. Then his face lit up. "I think I might know how we can pull it off."

He'd go with Frank and Joe to the exchange. Greg and Mike were to stay with their mother to guard against any attempt to take her again. Dunn would wait in the center of the platform, taking Frank's place, since he was the least athletic of the three. When the crooks arrived with Callie, Dunn would hand them the microfilm. While they were checking it, Joe and Frank would come charging in, creating a diversion that would let Dunn pull his gun and grab Callie.

"Of course, if it's clear they're on guard against a move like that, we won't try to pull it off," Dunn said.

"Right," said Frank. "We can't put Callie in any more danger than she's already in."

"If it looks like it won't come off, I'll drop my briefcase, as if by accident. That'll be your signal to hold back. They should just think I'm nervous."

"One thing still puzzles me," said Frank, working at figuring out all the angles. "What was this Clark guy doing with the microfilm in the first place?"

"Don't know. Maybe he was going to blackmail Rawley," said Dunn. "It wouldn't be the first time an employee tried to put the bite on his boss. Or he might have just found out about Rawley's secrets and been gathering evidence to turn him in to the authorities. Either way, Clark didn't figure how savage Rawley could be."

"I can hardly wait to get my hands on these guys," Joe said. "Starting with the kidnappers and going right up to the top. I'll show them savage."

But after a half hour of waiting in the dilapidated station, Joe was beginning to doubt that he and the others were going anywhere except back to Bayport empty-handed. He had virtually memorized the spray-painted graffiti that covered every inch of the grimy walls.

95

It had been at least half an hour since the last train had arrived, virtually empty. It had made its brief stop without anyone getting off, then rumbled away.

Now, in the distance, from far down the tracks, Joe heard the echoing rumble of another train approaching. He tensed. The kidnappers hadn't said how they'd arrive in this station, but after seeing how deserted the station was, Joe had a strong hunch they'd come by train. It would be the perfect way to get in and out fast.

The rumbling grew louder, and Joe leaned forward, his attention fixed on Dunn. When the train arrived and the kidnappers made their move, Joe would have to move faster than they could.

Then, abruptly, before the train made it to the station, the rumbling stopped.

The train was experiencing what the New York Transit Authority like to call "a temporary delay."

But if that was bad news for the passengers, it was good luck for Joe.

If the train had kept rumbling along, he never would have heard the footsteps coming up behind him.

He whirled around to face a man who stood with his arm upraised, about to bring a blackjack down on Joe's head. In that split second, Joe's brain registered that the man was dressed in a black jogging suit and black ski mask—just like the goons who had jumped him and Frank the night before.

But there was no time for Joe to think about it. There was just time for him to react.

His hand shot out and grabbed the attacker's wrist and gave it a sharp yank in the direction it was already moving. When the attacker was off balance, Joe wrenched his wrist again, and the blackjack dropped to the concrete platform.

Meanwhile, the rumble of the train had resumed. Joe, though, couldn't turn to see what was happening down the platform. He still had to deal with the masked goon, who had managed to twist his hand free and throw a right cross toward Joe's chin.

Joe blocked it with his left forearm and drove his own right deep into the goon's stomach. The masked man collapsed like a balloon losing air.

Joe followed his right with a left hook to the point of the goon's jaw.

A deep grunt emerged from the ski mask. The guy had a head like a rock, Joe thought angrily, and he lashed out with a right to the jaw, putting every ounce of his muscle behind it.

The goon shook his head again, as if he couldn't believe this was happening to him. He started to cock his fist as if Joe hadn't even touched him. Then slowly his fist turned limp and fell, and he crumpled slowly to the platform.

Joe didn't pause to savor his triumph. He

turned around fast—and saw that the doors of the train had finished closing, and the subway was moving away with a sudden burst of speed, as if to make up for the time lost by its delay.

At the same time, Joe saw something else—something that made him run to catch up with the departing train.

The platform was empty. Dunn and the microfilm were gone.

Then the train was gone too. Joe couldn't catch up with it.

He stood watching the rear light until it vanished in the darkness—until another thought hit him.

Frank.

He had never run faster than he did in making a dash for the other end of the platform where Frank had been stationed.

But even as he ran, he had a sinking feeling in his stomach.

The feeling was right.

Frank was gone too.

They had jumped him, dragged him away.

Joe didn't have time to check his attacker. He had to find a phone, call the Rawleys, warn them. He spotted one on the platform and raced for it. When he got to it, he saw the Out of Order sign.

Joe went up the subway stairs three at a time. He had to hunt for a phone out on the street, or maybe in an all-night grocery, if one was around.

He emerged from the subway and stood a moment, taking in deep lungfuls of cool night air. He looked around him, and down the deserted street he saw a phone booth. He ran to it, pulled open the door, and grabbed the receiver off the hook with one hand while he reached into his pocket for change with his other.

He had no hands free when he heard the booth door yanked open behind him.

He had only time enough to turn to see the recovered ski-masked goon standing there with one hand on the door handle and the other bunched into a fist heading straight for his jaw.

The fist seemed to explode in the center of Joe's brain, and Joe saw—nothing.

Nothing but shooting stars of pain in endless pitch-blackness!

Chapter

12

IT WAS ANIMAL instinct that made Joe grab his attacker's knees as he went down.

It was animal instinct—the will to survive—that made him tighten his grip and hold on as the attacker tried to kick himself free.

Joe's head began to clear.

With returning strength flooding through him with every beat of his heart, Joe pulled his attacker down.

Locked together, they rolled out onto the sidewalk.

Joe broke free of the attacker's hold on his head. He was on his feet a split second before the attacker managed to get on his.

The man in black never made it all the way up. Joe's hand chopped down on the back of his neck. Joe had to admit that the martial-arts training that Frank had pushed him into taking paid off now and then—and this was one of those times.

Panting, his head still slightly fuzzy, Joe tried to focus on what he should do next. But before he could, the question was answered for him. Another man in a black jogging suit and ski mask emerged from the subway, carrying a gun.

Unfortunately, the goon spotted Joe at the same time as Joe saw him.

Joe had to run for it. But he knew he couldn't run in a straight line. He could beat the guy in a flat-out race—Joe was the fastest running back in Bayport High history. But there was no way he could outrun a bullet.

Instead he ran weaving down the sidewalk until he reached the first alleyway and ducked into it.

He didn't go far down it, though. Instead he pressed himself flat against the wall near the entrance and waited.

The goon did exactly what Joe hoped he would. He ran into the alley in hot pursuit.

His gun was still drawn but he didn't get to use it. Because that was the first thing Joe took care of when he jumped him. Joe gave the guy's wrist a vicious chop, and the gun fell to the ground. Joe continued to hang on to him.

So far, so good—but then things that Joe hadn't planned on started happening.

The first thing was, the goon was bigger than Joe had thought. Bigger, and stronger. A lot stronger. And quick.

He shook Joe off like a dog shaking off water. He didn't bother bending down for his gun—he went after Joe with bare hands.

Joe put everything he had into a left jab, then a right cross—but his one-two added up to zero. The masked man merely shook his head as if a gnat had given him a slightly annoying bite, then he bore in on Joe.

His massive arms circled Joe in a powerful bear hug. Joe struggled for a second before he knew it was hopeless. The man's arms felt as if they were made of steel, and they were tightening like a vise. Already Joe couldn't breathe. In another couple of seconds, his ribs were going to crack. Joe didn't want to think what would happen after that.

There was only one thing Joe thought to try—a move he had never tried before.

He had seen it in kung fu movies and could only hope he had understood it.

Here goes nothing, he thought on the verge of blacking out.

He stretched his neck backward as a rattler would rear back before striking.

Then he brought his head forward so that his forehead bashed against the goon's.

In the shattering pain that followed, he only

had time for one thought: If the other guy's head is as hard as yours, which one of you goes down?

A security system can only be as good as the men running it. The guards at the building where Laser, Inc., had its offices were not very good. They were the kind of guards who would let any kid in, as long as they thought he was making a delivery.

The kid had a pizza box cradled in his arms and whined that he'd never get a tip if it was cold when he got upstairs. The guards were sure it was just another pizza for those idiot engineers up in the laser designs division, so they let him through. If they had checked what the box held, they would have realized then that their careers in the security business had just ended.

When the boy got to the thirty-second floor, he didn't stop at the laser lab. He went directly down the hall to the executive suites, cut the string on the pizza box, and opened it to reveal a very professional set of lock picks and a variety of other gadgets, both electronic and mechanical. It took the teenager only a moment to disable the security alarm and crack the lock on the presidential suite, and seconds after that he was standing in Walter Rawley's pitch-black office.

A tiny quartz halogen lamp in hand, the young man went through one drawer after another, scanned dozens of files, even spent some time on

Rawley's personal computer. As the office's floor-to-ceiling windows went from black to predawn gray, the young man clicked off the tiny lamp that had been his only company and looked about him as if still puzzled. There was a lot here, but there was a great deal more missing. And it was beginning to seem to him that the missing parts were about to turn into another puzzle entirely.

Joe woke in pitch-blackness. Then a dim circle of red appeared. Without opening his eyes, he knew where he was. He was lying on a beach, his eyes shut against the burning sun. He had a throbbing headache. The tide must be coming in. He felt the water lapping at his neck, his cheeks, his nose.

Then it was lapping at his eyelids, and he forced them open—to find himself staring into the eyes of a calico alley cat whose tongue had been industriously giving Joe's face the once-over. The cat exchanged stares with him a moment, then yawned, curved its spine high into the air, and walked away unhurriedly with its tail straight up for a second. Clearly finding someone unconscious in this alley wasn't anything new to it.

Joe sat up, the blood pounding in his head. Burning sunlight was streaming into the alley. He recalled a gun lying on the ground and looked for it. It was gone. It took him a minute more to discover that his wallet and keys were gone too, his pockets turned inside out. But it was only when he got to his feet that he realized something else was missing. His brand-new running shoes.

He looked at the goon lying at his feet and saw the guy was in his socks as well. Someone must have spotted them lying there in the alleyway. They were lucky to have the clothes on their backs. He walked on wobbly legs over to the prone body of his assailant and pulled off the man's ski mask. The face was completely unfamiliar. Probably pure rent-a-thug, he thought.

By now the shock of waking up battered and robbed was wearing off, and even more painful and important thoughts were popping into Joe's head.

Dunn and the microfilm were now in the crooks' hands along with Callie.

Frank had been jumped by a goon and was now missing. Maybe Frank had been captured, but maybe it was even worse than that.

What really hurt was that right then there was nothing Joe could do to help any of them.

All he could do was what he had been trying to do when the goon yanked him away from the phone. He had to contact Mrs. Rawley and Greg and Mike and tell them what had happened so they could be ready.

Gingerly Joe stepped over some broken glass in the alley and out onto the sunlit Sunday-morning street. Battered, shoeless, his jeans and shirt covered with grime, he looked pitiful. In the distance he saw the telephone he had tried to use the night before. To his relief he saw that the receiver had not been torn off in the scuffle the night before. Joe sped up his pace. Just a quick phone call and then . . .

"Hello, operator? I want to make a collect call. . . ." Joe realized he was speaking to dead air. He hung up, then picked up the receiver again and punched *0*.

"No," Joe moaned, slamming the receiver down. Of course, it was one of those new pay-before-you-play phones. Where was he going to get phone money?

Then he heard a voice that seemed like the answer to his prayers.

"Hey, fellas, who wants to make an easy quarter?"

Joe turned in the direction of the voice and saw that it came from a concrete school yard. There, beneath a rusted basketball hoop whose net had long been torn away, a group of teenagers had gathered. One of them, a long stringbean of a guy who looked like he was on his way to a basketball scholarship and an NBA contract, was standing bouncing a basketball.

As Joe headed toward them, he could hear the tall kid saying derisively, "I thought you guys were sports. Come on, you don't even have to play me one-on-one if you don't want. We can just shoot fouls. First one misses, he loses a quarter. What could be fairer than that?"

One of the kids around him answered, "Come on, Wes, what do you take us for? We ain't fools. I got better ways to lose my change."

By now Joe had reached the group.

"I hear you offer a quarter?" he said.

Wes's face lit up in a big grin. "My *man*. Be the easiest quarter you ever made. All you got to do is shoot fouls better than me, and everybody knows I can hardly hold a ball, let alone shoot it."

As he said this, he flipped the ball over his shoulder in the most casual hook shot Joe had ever seen. It went through the basket without touching the rim, while the crowd of kids broke into loud guffaws.

Joe shrugged. "What do I have to lose?" he said with a shrug.

"Just a quarter," said Wes, and his eyes narrowed with suspicion. "You do have a quarter, don't you?"

"Sure I do," said Joe. "You want to see it in advance?"

"Won't be necessary," Wes said. "Just so I see it afterward. You don't look overly blessed with brains, but I don't figure you're dumb enough to bet what you don't have. That would be one dumb move."

He slapped one huge fist into his palm. As if that weren't enough, some of his friends in the crowd made the same gesture. A few of them looked as if they'd just as soon have Joe *not* pay.

"Come on, man, stop trying to mess up my head and shoot the ball," said Joe, trying to keep his heart out of his throat.

"Just so you know the rules," said Wes, taking the ball and standing with his toes touching a line painted on the concrete. "First I shoot, then you. First one to miss hands over the silver. No credit. No double-or-nothing. Understood?"

"Understood," Joe said, and watched Wes sight briefly, then arc the ball easily through the hoop.

"Your turn, hotshot," Wes said, sending the ball on one hard bounce to Joe as he stepped up to the line.

Last basketball season, Joe had won the district championship for Bayport High by sinking a foul shot in the closing seconds of double-overtime, after a game where he had scored his career high. The school paper had called it the shot of his life after the game of his life.

Right now, though, as he sighted the basket, he didn't feel as if he was going after the shot of his life. It was more like the shot *for* his life.

His life, and the lives of others.

Linda Rawley. Greg Rawley. Mike Rawley.

Not to mention Dunn and Callie and, of course, Frank, if they were still alive.

The basket looked tiny as a star in the night sky and just as far away. The basketball felt as heavy as lead. His muscles felt like water.

"Come on, man, *shoot*," Wes said, his voice a rasping snarl designed to rub what was left of Joe's nerves raw. "A quarter can't mean that much to you." His voice grew even nastier. "Or *can* it?"

Joe wasn't sure who shot the ball. It certainly didn't seem as if he had.

He felt like a spectator sitting off to one side, watching a stranger shoot the ball and following the ball's flight. It seemed to arc through the air forever, rising in slow motion and then descending—right through the hoop.

Joe started breathing again.

"Your turn, Wes," he said, finding his voice.

Wes shrugged contemptuously. He grabbed the ball and shot. Through the hoop.

Joe's turn again. This time it was easier. Through the hoop.

Wes. Another basket.

Joe. He was into it now. He didn't even think of missing. Basket.

Wes nodded appreciatively. His sneer was gone. But his confidence was still there. He grinned at Joe and said, "Not bad, but won't be good enough.'' He raised the ball in his hands, ready to send it through the hoop again.

Then, just as he was getting the shot off, it happened. A bottle, flung out a window, smashed on the concrete. It sounded as loud as a stick of dynamite. Wes's shot hit the rim and bounded off at a crazy angle.

If Joe had on a hat, he would have taken it off to Wes. The guy didn't complain. He just gave a shrug and tossed the ball to Joe.

In another situation, Joe might have deliberately missed his next shot to be fair.

Not now, though.

He sighted very carefully, then shot.

But even thinking about missing had thrown him off.

His shot, too, hit the rim.

It bounded straight up into the air—then dropped through the hoop.

Wes flipped him a quarter and said, ''Okay, let's go at it again.''

Joe hated to say it, but did so anyway. ''Sorry. I'm quitting while I'm ahead.''

Wes gave a grimace of disgust. ''You sure aren't from this neighborhood, man,'' he said, grinning, but his contempt was clear as he left the school yard.

Joe would have liked to explain, but he didn't have time.

He, too, left the school yard and headed back

down the street to the pay phone. Quickly he dropped in the quarter, punched the *0* for the operator, and had her call Callie's number collect.

The phone rang three times, then Linda Rawley answered. Her voice sounded tense.

"Who is it?"

Joe heard the operator say, "A Mr. Joe Hardy calling you collect from New York. Will you accept the call?"

"Yes, please, put him on quickly," she said.

"You may talk to your party now," the operator told Joe.

"Mrs. Rawley, what's wrong?" Joe asked.

"They're closing in," she said, her voice frantic. "You have to—"

Her voice was cut off. There was a buzzing noise. Someone had broken the connection, either by hanging up the phone or by cutting the line.

Joe bit his lip. He had to get back to Bayport fast to find out what was going on. Somehow he had to dig up the subway and train fare, since without his keys there was no way he could use his van, even if he could persuade the attendant at the parking lot where he had left it to trust him for the fee.

He turned away from the phone only to find Wes, king of the concrete court, staring him in the face.

"What's the matter?" the dark giant said as he straightened up to his full height. "You look like somebody just ran over your dog." He took a long slow sip from the can of soda in his hand.

"I don't have a dog," Joe said nervously as he glanced down both ends of the street. No escape there. "But I do have troubles. Lots of them, and I hope you're not going to add to them." Joe tensed, ready to fight if he had to, hoping that he could just walk away.

A quick grin lit Wes's face and was followed by deep laughter. "I got troubles enough too, without having to look for any new ones." His face got serious again. "So why don't you chill out. Tell me a little story."

Joe felt some of the tension in his shoulders leave, and then, to his surprise, heard himself telling Wes the whole story. He watched the other youth's eyes light up, his head nod in understanding. As the story tumbled out faster and faster he even found himself hoping that he had a chance to get back before it was too late.

Chapter

13

THE SPRUNG CAB that rumbled through the Bayport streets looked totally out of place. The windows were rolled down, letting ear-splitting salsa music blare out at the residents for blocks around. A dog barked furiously at the cab from his fenced-in, manicured lawn as the rusty Dodge, with its wired-on muffler and dragging fender, pulled up a block from Callie's house.

"Thanks for the ride, Wes. And the shoes," Joe said, pointing to the pair of worn-out black high-tops. "I'll pay you back soon, I promise."

"I know you will, man," said Wes, looking around at the neat lawns with an expression of wry amusement. "After all, you're from the *suburbs*."

"Come on, you back there, I ain't got all day,"

said the cabbie, a fat, unshaven man who was smoking a cigarette as he nervously tapped the steering wheel to the beat of the music. "The cops'll throw me in jail for just parking in this neighborhood."

"Yeah, yeah, Tony. He's going, he's going." Wes turned to Joe. "Rich people make my friends nervous."

Joe smiled. "So, maybe we'll meet again," he said, offering his hand. "On the courts, I mean."

"Maybe." Wes grinned as Joe got out of the car, glancing worriedly toward Callie's house. "But I'll bet you two bits, next time you see me on the court you'll have to buy a ticket to do it."

"Unless I'm on the team too," Joe couldn't help adding.

Wes closed the door of the rickety car. He leaned out the window as the cab pulled away from the curb. "Let me leave you with a word of advice, Joe."

"What's that?" Joe asked, instantly alert.

Wes grinned. "Keep your eye on the ball."

With a screech of tires, the cab made a U-turn in the street and disappeared around a corner, loud music lingering in its wake. Joe shook his head. Wes had turned out to be a really great guy. It was a shame they couldn't have shot a few more rounds of ball together. But Joe had work to do.

He headed toward Callie's house, trying not to

trip in the high-tops, which were a little too big for him and nearly worn through.

Joe reached Callie's house and started to press the front doorbell. But before he could, the door swung open.

"Quick, get inside," Greg Rawley said.

Joe followed instructions. As soon as he had entered, Greg slammed shut the door and double-locked it.

"I see you're keeping a sharp lookout," Joe said as he went with Greg into the living room. Linda Rawley and Mike were there. Mike was standing by the window, peering out through a narrow opening in the closed blinds.

"There have been a couple of guys keeping watch on this place," said Greg. "They tried to stay out of sight, but we spotted them. We were going to call the cops to complain about suspicious characters, figuring that would get rid of them without endangering Callie, but you phoned just as we were about to make the call. Then the line went dead. They must have cut it. Which leaves us trapped in here. I'm surprised they let you get in."

"I'm not," said Joe. "I'm in the same trap you're in now. They can take us all at once when they get ready."

"Maybe they'll wait until Frank gets here too," Greg said. "Where is he, anyway?"

Joe bit his lip. "I wish I knew." He had to

pause before he could go on, his voice grim. "They jumped us both. I got away, but Frank didn't. They must be holding him now, along with Callie. Unless—" He paused again. "But I don't want to think about that. I can't think that he might be—" Joe couldn't bring himself to say the word. But the bleak look in his eyes said it all.

"And Dunn?" asked Linda Rawley.

"They grabbed him too," Joe reported. "Pulled him aboard a subway train."

"They're chewing us up, one by one," said Mike, still peering out the window. "We were outnumbered to start with, and the odds keep getting worse and worse."

"There're so many of them—and now there're only four of us," Linda Rawley said, agreeing.

"If only there was some way to cut down the odds," Greg said glumly. Then his face brightened. There was a spark of excitement in his voice. "But maybe there is."

"You've got a plan?" asked Mike, brightening too.

"Tell us," Linda Rawley implored eagerly, the taut, almost haggard look on her pretty face fading in a sudden glow of hope.

"The thing is, it's very dangerous and it all depends on Joe here," said Greg.

Joe's answer was instant. "I'd rather risk my life doing something than just wait here doing nothing."

*   *   *

Six hours later, after nightfall, Joe was thinking, Maybe I should have shot this plan down. I could wind up getting hurt.

But when Greg had asked him if he was ready, Joe had made his voice cheerful. "Ready, willing, and eager."

They were standing at the back door. Greg shouted through the house to Mike, who was standing at the front door.

"Okay, Mike, *go!*"

Silently Greg and Joe counted to five in unison. Joe pictured Mike going out the front door on the run, moving as fast as Joe had seen him go on the gridiron. But now he had to dodge any bullets that might come flying at him.

"Five," whispered Greg. *"Go, Joe!"*

Joe moved away quickly from the back door. He hoped that Mike had managed to divert the attention of the guys watching the house. Mike then had to get back inside the house safely after pretending to abandon his attempt to break out. Then he forgot about Mike. What he had to worry about was himself as he dashed across the back lawn.

Good thing there was no moon. Still, the light from neighboring houses and a distant streetlight did give more illumination than he liked. But at least that light worked both ways. He was able to

117

see a couple of men dashing ahead of him before they saw him.

He hit the ground and lay flat against it. The pair of men stopped nearby.

"See, I told you nobody was coming out the back door," said one, panting and trying to catch his breath.

"Lucky for you," gasped the other, sucking in air. "You were told not to abandon your post here, no matter what."

"You sounded like you needed help in front," the first said, protesting.

"That move could have been a trick," said the second. "Oldest trick in the world. That kid dashing out, drawing fire, then ducking back inside the house."

"Naw," said the first man contemptuously. "He was just scared out of his pants. These silencers may keep the neighbors from hearing shots, but I guarantee you when he heard a few bullets whistle by, he realized real fast that this wasn't a game. That put a stop to that hero stuff. Like the boss said, they're all amateurs in there."

"Well, he should know," said the second. "I mean, he's married to one, plays dad to the other two, and he's been like some kind of uncle to the two Hardy kids."

Lying pressed against the ground, Joe grimaced. Any doubts he had about Walter Rawley

118

were gone now—and so was his last lingering hesitation about what he had to do.

Joe lay motionless, his muscles coiled for action, while the second crook said, "I'm heading out front again. You stay here, and keep a sharp lookout."

"Yeah, sure, but they're too scared to do anything," said the other man.

Then, after the second crook had left, Joe made his move.

He made it short and sweet.

He was on his feet and throwing a punch at the man's jaw in one lightning motion. The guy never knew what hit him. He went down like a sack of potatoes.

Joe stood over him, rubbing his knuckles.

"Good to see I haven't lost my touch," he said to himself, enjoying the same kind of triumphant feeling he had had sinking baskets in the city. Then that glow faded as he thought of the job ahead. Now comes the hard part, he thought.

Fifteen minutes later, jogging all the way, he arrived at the Rawleys' house.

Standing at the front door, he hesitated a moment, then steeled himself and pressed the buzzer.

Walter P. Rawley answered the door himself.

"Joe, what are you doing here?" he asked surprised.

"I have to talk to you—alone," said Joe, making his voice sound desperate.

"You can do that here," said Walter Rawley. "My wife's not here right now and I don't know where Greg and Mike are. Probably out in that convertible of theirs, cruising. Come on in and let's talk."

As soon as the door had closed behind him, Joe said, "Your wife and sons, I've just seen them."

"But you couldn't have," Walter Rawley said in a stunned voice. "They've been—" Then he paused.

"You don't have to keep it a secret," Joe said. "I know. They've been kidnapped. They told me."

"But how? Why?" said Walter Rawley, sounding amazed.

"Your sons got Frank and me involved in the case," Joe explained. "We found your wife and helped her escape. But your sons were captured right after. They escaped too, and they're all hiding out at Callie Shaw's house. Except that now the house is surrounded."

"But why didn't you tell me about all this before?" Walter Rawley demanded.

"This is kind of hard to say," said Joe, sounding embarrassed, "but Mrs. Rawley and Greg and Mike made us promise not to tell you. They had a crazy idea you were involved in some kind of funny business. In fact, they actually thought you were behind the kidnappings for a while. Of course, Frank and I knew better. I mean, we've known you for so much longer than they have. The idea of you being a crook is completely crazy. But we had to go along with their demand to keep you out of our investigation if we wanted to stay on the case. So we said okay. But the crooks are closing in on them now again. And I figured it was time to turn to you for help. You're the best one—the only one—to decide what to do now."

"You did absolutely right, Joe," Walter Rawley said, putting his hand on Joe's shoulder. "Good work. Your father will be proud of you when I tell him about this. But first I'll get Linda and the boys out of their jam. I'm finally free to do what I've wanted to from the very first. I'm going to call the police. You wait right here."

Joe looked into Walter Rawley's face, the gentle, kindly face he had known since he was a kid, no hint of malice or deception on it. Then Joe thought, I just bet you're going to call the cops. What a good actor you've been all these years.

Then Joe did the hardest thing he had ever done in his life.

As Walter Rawley withdrew his hand from Joe's shoulder and was about to turn away to go to the phone in the living room, Joe lashed out with his right hand. It was like shooting fish in a

121

barrel. He connected square on Walter Rawley's jaw, and the older man went down.

But Joe felt as if he were the one who had been punched—right in the stomach. He felt dizzy, almost sick.

Get hold of yourself, he told himself. Act like a pro. It had to be done. Walter Rawley was playing you for a sucker and you know it. If you hadn't knocked him out, he would have called in his goons and rubbed you out and then finished off the others.

The trouble was, knowing all this didn't make him feel any better. He had to force himself to continue with the plan, feeling sick all the while.

He reached in Walter Rawley's pocket and found his car keys. Then he frisked Rawley and found something else in his jacket pocket. A .32 automatic.

"It figures," he thought, and felt better about what he had done. The guy was deadly as a rattler.

Getting a glass of water from the kitchen, Joe splashed it in Rawley's face. When Rawley came to, he found himself staring into the barrel of his own gun.

Joe didn't like the feel of the gun in his hand. Guns definitely were not his thing. And he knew that there was no way he could ever pull the trigger on Walter Rawley, no matter what Rawley had done. Hitting Rawley was just about the hardest thing he had ever done. Shooting him was simply impossible.

But he couldn't let Rawley know that. And Joe didn't figure that Rawley would call his bluff.

All Rawley could do was assume a puzzled, confused tone. "Joe, what happened? What's wrong?"

"No talk—just do what I say or pay the price," Joe said. He made his voice menacing. He wasn't sure he'd trust himself to resist Walter Rawley, if Rawley started appealing to him.

The sight of the gun silenced Rawley. With a stunned look on his face, he let Joe march him to the car. On Joe's command, he sat in the driver's seat while Joe sat beside him.

Joe inserted the car keys, turned on the ignition, and ordered Rawley to drive to within a block of Callie's house. When they arrived, Joe made him get out. He marched him at gunpoint to where they could approach the house from the rear.

"Not a sound," Joe warned him, and Rawley nodded. He still looked stunned. Joe could see that he couldn't get over the fact that he had been outsmarted. Rawley had been playing a winning hand so long that he had forgotten what it was like to lose.

"When the guy guarding the rear spots us, just wave to him, like there's nothing wrong," Joe told him. "I'm putting the gun in the pocket of my jacket but I'm keeping the safety off and my finger on the trigger. Make one false move and it will be your last one."

"But—" Rawley started to protest.

"Save your breath, if you want to keep breathing," Joe said harshly. "Just do what I say."

Rawley shrugged and nodded his head, a defeated look on his face.

He didn't have to do a thing, though, when the thug at the rear of the house spotted them. The man moved toward them menacingly, but when he saw it was Rawley, he stood aside respectfully and let them pass.

When they reached the rear door, Joe wasn't surprised to see it swing open before he had to knock. He could imagine how the three inside must have been waiting and watching, hoping that he had pulled this off.

He saw he was right. The faces of Linda Rawley and her sons lit up with triumph as they gathered around him and his prisoner.

What Joe wasn't expecting, though, was that Walter Rawley's face would light up too.

"Linda. Greg. Mike. You're alive, thank God," he exclaimed.

"He'd make a great actor, wouldn't he, Joe?" Greg said with a sneer.

"He certainly would have fooled me," Joe admitted. "In fact, he has for all these years."

He pulled the gun out of his pocket and handed

it to Greg. "You take this. You can take charge of the rest of this. I don't have the heart for it."

"Gee, thanks," said Greg. "Though actually we don't need it."

"Yeah," said Mike, pulling out a gun of his own, an imposing-looking .45.

"Still, you've made our job a little bit simpler," said Linda Rawley, smiling and lighting a cigarette while her sons leveled their guns.

"Yeah, and we'll give you a reward for your good work," said Greg, with a nasty grin turning his boyish good looks into something older and ugly. "You can have a choice. Who should we knock off first, our dear stepdad or our good pal, *you*?"

Chapter

14

Now Joe knew why Walter Rawley looked so stunned, so confused, so bewildered.

Joe felt exactly the same way.

"Hey, this some kind of joke? If it is, let me in on it," was all he could say. But even as he said it, he knew that Greg wasn't joking. Greg and Mike looked too comfortable with guns in their hands. And the quiet nasty smiles on their faces told him who the real actors had been all along.

"He wants to be let in on the joke," Greg said to his brother. "Think we should do him a favor?"

"Too bad Frank isn't here," said Mike in the same sneering tone. "Maybe he could have figured it all out."

"What say we give Joe here a chance to show

us what a brilliant detective he is on his own," said Mike.

"Come on, no fooling around," Linda Rawley said harshly. "We have to get this over with fast. It feels like I've been on this job forever. You kids just had to be here a couple of months. I've had to play house for so long that I feel like I should be fetching Walter his slippers."

"Aw, Mom," said Greg in a tone of mock protest. "Boys just want to have fun."

"I'm beginning to understand," said Joe as the whole ugly picture became clear to him.

"So am I," said Walter Rawley grimly.

"You've been playing a role, all this time, ever since we first met," he said, looking directly at his wife.

"Congratulations, Walter," she replied sarcastically, snuffing out a cigarette even as she lit another. "Understanding is the key to a good marriage."

"I should have known it was too good to be true when I met you on that trip to California," Rawley went on. "The way you accidentally tripped and spilled your drink on me at that restaurant. The way you insisted on my sending you the bill for dry cleaning my suit jacket and invited me to have a drink with you after dinner by way of apology. The way you were so sympathetic about how lonely I was ever since the death of my wife and the way you told me how lonely you were too. It seemed so natural for us to see each other again, and then again, and even more natural for me to ask you to marry me. It happened almost before I knew I was going to do it.''

"Yeah, I was good," Linda Rawley said, blowing out a puff of smoke. "Maybe I should have stuck to being an actress instead of going into this line of work. But the money was so hard to turn down, even though I do miss the applause.''

"But, *why?*" Rawley asked, his expression pained. "I gave you all you asked for—money, clothes, a home for yourself and your sons, social position." He paused, then added bitterly, "Not to mention my love.''

"Yeah, all that was pretty nice, but it wasn't quite enough," Linda said. "See, my bosses offered me even more than what you gave me. And they play real rough with anyone who doesn't give them what they ask for. So I had to get what they wanted, and what they wanted was everything.''

Walter Rawley knew at once what she was talking about. "Of course. That will you had me write, after Greg and Mike arrived. You said you weren't concerned about yourself, but you were worried about their future, if anything ever happened to me. So you asked me to put in writing what I already had told you. If I died, you inherited everything." He shook his head at the memory. "I suppose they really aren't even your kids."

"Why, stepfather, how can you even think that?" said Greg.

"You can see how well she raised us," said Mike. "We're carrying on a family tradition."

"Yeah, a whole family of bad actors," muttered Joe.

"Well, we fooled you, man," Mike said.

"And your bright brother too," said Greg. "He was really going crazy with jealousy when I started acting friendly with that Callie chick. I figured that would give him the extra push he needed to want to show her what a great detective he was."

"But why did you want to get Frank and me involved?" Joe asked. "Wasn't that asking for trouble?"

Greg gave a nasty chuckle. "You overestimate how good you and your brother are. You two were putty in our hands."

"But that doesn't answer my question, *why* did you want to use us?" Joe asked again, though he already could make a guess.

"You like to think you're so smart, why don't you tell us?" Mike said, taunting him. "Go ahead, speedy, I'll give you the ball and see how far you can run with it."

Joe paused while his ideas took shape. He started speaking hesitantly, but his words came swifter and surer as more and more pieces of the puzzle fit together.

"You wanted to be able to get rid of Mr. Rawley, and had to find a way to do it so that you wouldn't be suspected," he said. "So you cooked up the story about his being involved with spies because of the top-secret work his company does for the government. And then you suggested he killed his first wife when she found out. You figured you could knock him off and say it was self-defense, because he was trying to kill you, his second wife and two stepsons, who had found out about his guilt."

"My God, is this true?" Walter Rawley gasped. "It's unbelievable."

"That was the trouble, a lot of people would never believe it," Joe went on. "Especially not my dad. The two of you have been friends for so long he wouldn't rest until he knew the truth." Joe shook his head as everything became absolutely clear to him. "But say Frank and I backed up the story. Say we actually thought we had uncovered all the facts on our own. *That* would have convinced my dad when Linda Rawley or Greg or Mike said they had had to kill Mr. Rawley in some kind of 'confrontation.' " Joe turned to Linda Rawley and her sons. "So you led Frank and me to find proof of Mr. Rawley's guilt so we'd testify to your innocence."

"Touchdown." Mike grinned. "Too bad Frank

isn't around to hear you. But I'm afraid Frank is out of the ball game now.''

"Yeah," said Greg. "Poor Callie. She'll be real upset when she hears about it. Maybe I'll try to console her. It'll be a way to pass the time while I wait for the investigation to end and Mom to get her hands on the company."

Joe fought down a feeling of disgust at the idea of a slimeball like Greg worming his way into Callie's affections. He fought down the sick feeling he had when he thought about what had happened to Frank. He had more pressing matters to deal with. Matters of life and death.

"But what happens to your grand plan now?" he demanded. "You don't have Frank to testify that Mr. Rawley is a murderer, and you don't have me. And you know that there's no way my dad is going to buy your story without us. You guys better figure out a new scam, because this one is shot full of holes."

"The only things that're going to be shot full of holes are Walter and you," said Greg with a smirk. "It was real nice of stepdaddy to bring his own gun. That'll make it all the more convincing when he's found with it in his hand. He'll be lying right near you, Joe. We'll put a gun in your hand too. Your dad will understand why you had to use it. He'll be proud of the way you died in a shoot-out defending us when the evil Walter Rawley burst in here to finish us off."

"And you really think he'll believe that story coming from you?" Joe said scornfully.

"Not from *us,* bright boy," said Mike. "But he will from a straight arrow like Callie. You see, Dunn is going to manage to find her and rescue her from the room where she's been locked up. Getting her involved in the case was Greg's idea, and it was a goodie. Since we have her to testify, we don't need you or your late, great brother."

"Don't look so glum," Greg said to Joe. "The spot you're in isn't bad. It's just hopeless."

Walter Rawley was still shaking his head in disbelief.

Linda Rawley saw it and smiled. "What's the matter, honey, you still have problems figuring out what's going down?" she said with mock sweetness. "I'm surprised, a big, brilliant executive like you."

"You've always hated me this much?" said Walter Rawley sadly.

"Now, Walter, don't be upset," Linda Rawley said. "You *are* kind of boring, but you're not so bad. There's nothing personal about this, it's just a job."

"And I can make a good guess who hired you, Mrs. Rawley," said Joe. "Somebody who wants to get his hands on Laser, Incorporated, who wants to find out what work Laser is doing for the Defense Department and who would love to have access to all the company's secrets."

Walter Rawley nodded. "Of course. Now it all makes sense. *They'd* have the resources to set up an elaborate operation like this. And you're right, the Russians would pay dearly for one *look* at our laser projects, and the chance to *own* one of the companies working on lasers would be worth billions to them."

"I'm glad you two have come up with all the answers," said Greg. "Because the question-and-answer period is over. There's only one more thing you have to know."

"What's that?" asked Joe. Although he was tired of this game, he was in no hurry to have it end.

"Our bosses are very impatient," said Greg. "Which is why you don't have any more time before you die."

Chapter

15

JOE STARED AT the gun pointed at his heart. Then, suddenly, he knew what he had to do.

Clutching his stomach, he doubled over, as if in intense pain.

Walter Rawley had seen the same thing Joe had. And he doubled over too.

What they both had seen was Frank Hardy sneaking into the living room behind Linda, Greg, and Mike. He signaled Joe and Walter Rawley to stage some kind of diversion.

They did—and it had worked.

"What the—?" was all Greg had a chance to say before Frank's arm snaked around his neck. Frank's free hand grabbed Greg's gun, wrestled it away, and tossed it aside.

As soon as Joe saw Mike begin to turn to help

Greg, Joe charged. A vicious chop to Mike's wrist sent his gun flying, and the two stood a moment, frozen, facing each other, each looking for an opening through which to strike.

Beside them, Greg broke free of Frank's hold and wheeled around to face him. Both his hands were turned into flat striking instruments as he assumed a karate posture.

"I hear you got a brown belt," he snarled. "Well, I got a black. So it's bye-bye time for you, Frankie boy."

Then, without a pause, he let out a piercing attack shriek and lashed out with his foot, while his hand cocked for a finishing chop.

Frank didn't recoil. He didn't even blink. As calmly as if the fight were in slow motion—though both boys were moving like lightning—Frank caught Greg's foot, flipped it—and Greg—up. Before Greg could recover, Frank delivered a stunning chop to the side of the neck that laid Greg out cold.

It was all over in an instant. Frank stood over him, looking down. "Pride and anger have no place in a fight, old pal. They make you blind. They make you lose."

Mike saw his brother down, Frank untouched, and Joe with his fist clenched ready to swing. It was easy for him to figure out the odds. Swiftly he made his move. He turned and ran.

Joe was after him in a flash—and brought him

down with a flying tackle before he made it to the door.

"Never thought you belonged in the back-field," Joe panted as he hauled an unresisting Mike to his feet and shoved him against the wall. "You'd have quit as soon as the score was against you."

At that moment Walter Rawley exclaimed, "Not so fast, my dear."

And he beat Linda to the guns on the floor, scooping up the one nearest to him. He held it on her while he picked up the other.

"Sorry, Linda," he said, his voice hard. "But it's no more Mr. Nice Guy."

A couple of minutes later Greg and Mike were also under Walter Rawley's gun. And Joe was able to say to Frank, "You could have shown up a little sooner. I was actually beginning to worry. And, oh, yeah, by the way, where did you disappear to? And where did you come from?"

Frank returned his brother's grin. "Sorry, Joe, that I wasn't able to let you in on what I was doing. But things started happening too fast, and I had to think and act even faster."

"Well, let me in on it now—starting with when you vanished in that subway station," said Joe. It was just like Frank, he thought, to make a mystery of a mystery, just so he could provide the solution in lavish detail.

"Actually, it started before I was jumped in

136

at station," said Frank. "It was nothing I could ut my finger on, but ever since you said the case elt too easy, I'd had my doubts about the whole etup. Evidence never stacks up as neatly as it id in this case—first from Greg and Mike, then om Linda, then from Dunn, then from the attack on Clark. It was almost as if someone was teering us in one direction. I mean, we didn't eally have to *work*. I kept feeling less and less ke a detective, and more and more like a puppet. hen, when I was jumped in the subway, it was ke a string snapped. I suddenly saw things from different angle and knew there were some questions that needed answers."

"Then they didn't get you?" said Joe.

"I spotted the goon coming out of the shadows ust in time," said Frank.

"Just like I did," said Joe.

"Yeah, I saw you struggling after I knocked y man out, but you seemed to have things under ontrol. So I tied my guy up, dropped him in a)umpster, and took off," said Frank. "I figured they had to hunt down two of us going in ifferent directions it would increase both our hances. Besides, I figured the less you knew bout what I was doing, the better, in case they aught you and tried to get it out of you."

"Thanks loads, brother dear," said Joe. Then e added, "You may have been right, but did you ave to leave all the goons on my trail?"

"Well, Joe," Frank said, grinning, "I figured you could handle it."

"Your father's told me you're quite a sleuth," said Walter Rawley. "But how did you figure out that I was innocent? They had both Joe and me fooled until a few minutes ago."

"Dad once told us that if a case feels wrong, it may be," Frank said quietly. "And if it's wrong, you should turn it every way but loose."

He looked at Rawley, a grin lighting up his face. "What I did was turn the case upside down. I tried to imagine what it would be like if you were the innocent one and your wife and kids the villains. All of a sudden a whole lot of things made sense. Right about then I really needed to talk to you but I wasn't entirely certain that I was right. So I did the next best thing—I dressed up like a delivery boy and broke into your office. I was looking for any evidence that would tie you to the Swiss bank account, secrets being sold, security leaks, anything that I could check my assumptions against."

For a moment Walter Rawley looked shocked, even angry, then he began to return Frank's smile. "Find anything interesting, son?"

"I realized right away that there was a lot going on at Laser that would be invaluable to our enemies," said Frank. "And that's when I began suspecting just who our opponents were. I made one phone call to Chief Daniels of the New York

Police Department, an old friend of ours, to check Dunn's detective license. When he came up empty, the whole house of cards came tumbling down.''

"So you had the police round up Dunn and his gang," Walter Rawley said.

Frank looked embarrassed. "Well, not exactly. You see, they still had Callie in their hands, and—"

At this point Greg couldn't resist crowing, "And you didn't want to risk endangering her. You are soft on that chick, aren't you? Well, remember, in case you're thinking of turning us in, if we go, she dies."

"But none of us want things to go that far, do we, Frank?" Linda chimed in, her voice a soft contrast to Greg's hard one. "I'm sure we can arrange some kind of a deal. A trade. You let us free and give us, say, twenty-four hours to clear out, and you'll get Callie back."

"Yeah, what good will putting us away do, if you never see Callie again?" Mike asked.

Joe couldn't believe what he saw in his brother's eyes. Something he had never seen there before. He saw doubt—and hesitation.

"Hey, Frank, you can't trust these characters to hand Callie back," he cautioned.

"We can't let them get away with this," said Walter Rawley.

"Think of what they did to Mr. Rawley's secretary, that Clark guy," said Joe. "It would be letting them get away with murder."

"They killed Clark?" said Walter Rawley incredulously.

"Yeah, and planted some phony evidence against you in his house," said Joe.

"Which is all the proof you need of what will happen to Callie if you make the wrong decision," said Greg, his voice venomous. He looked Frank straight in the eyes, and Frank had to turn his eyes away.

"Let me think a minute," said Frank, biting his lip.

"Come on, Frank," Joe pleaded. "Think of these crooks laughing when they get away scot-free."

"Think of Callie, man," said Greg. "Think how pretty she is. Think how nice she is. And then think how dead she'll be."

"I need time," Frank said, almost shouting.

"Time is what you don't have. Callie's time is running out."

Frank's shoulders slumped. He looked defeated. As Joe and Mr. Rawley listened, mute with shock, he said wearily, "Okay, you win. Let's set up the trade."

Linda, Greg, and Mike all let their breath out in one giant sigh of relief.

"I'll call John right now and set things in motion," Linda said. She went to the phone, picked it up, and dialed. She listened a moment, then took her mouth away from the receiver long enough to say, "Nobody answers. I'll have to leave a message on his machine." She spoke into the phone. "The Hardy kids are on to us. But they're willing to exchange us for Callie. Call us as quick as you can and we'll work out the details." She hung up and said, "We'll have to wait—but we won't have to wait long. John moves fast."

"John moves even faster than you think," said a voice from the doorway.

Everyone in the room turned to see John Dunn standing there.

In one hand was the .45 that the boys had seen before, but in the other was something much more frightening—a radio-controlled detonator.

"Hello, Walter," he said menacingly. "Just drop your gun. If I push this button, a very lovely young lady will be blown sky-high."

His expression grim, Walter Rawley stood motionless for one long minute, then he clicked the pistol's safety on and dropped it, soundlessly, onto the carpet at his feet. Frank let out a long sigh of relief.

"I got here just in time to hear your message, Linda," John Dunn said. "You did a nice bit of negotiating, but I'm happy to say it was unnecessary. We can forget about trading now. We don't have to give up anything to get everything we want.''

He didn't have to say anything more. The big smile on his face said it all.

Chapter

16

"DAD, I KNEW you'd come through," Greg said.

"Don't I always?" Dunn said. He draped his left arm affectionately around his son's shoulder.

" 'Dad'?" said Joe, his mouth falling open. "You mean—?"

Walter Rawley's expression was even more stunned.

"Sure, it makes perfect sense," Frank said. "The family that slays together, stays together. Right, John, or whatever your real name is?"

"You have the answer as usual, bright boy." Dunn grinned. "Too bad you didn't wise up sooner. It wasn't too smart of you to call and tell me you were heading here. But, of course, as far as you were concerned I was on your team. Well, don't feel bad, Frankie. We all make mistakes. Too bad for you this one will be your last.''

A troubled look came over Greg's face. There was a note of urgency in his voice. "Dad, when did Frank call you to tell you where he was going?"

Dunn looked puzzled at his son's concern. "Why, just a few hours ago. He left a message on my machine. He said he hoped I had escaped from the crooks the same way he had, and that he was heading back to Bayport to make sure the three of us were still safe at Callie's."

There was panic in Greg's voice as he said, "Dad, maybe you didn't get there in time to hear, but Frank told us that he already *knew* about you by that time. Why would he let you in on his plans then?"

Suddenly Dunn looked worried too. He pointed his gun at Frank meaningfully. "Okay, Frank, explain and explain fast."

But Frank didn't have to.

Something else happened fast—faster than Dunn could react to. Bill Hooper and Chet Morton came tearing through the doorway behind him.

Biff hit Dunn low, Chet hit him high.

Just Biff alone would have brought Dunn down. If he hadn't been such a great fullback, he would have made a star tackle. And with Chet's added weight, Dunn went down like a pancake being

144

squashed. Chet, another of the Hardy's inner circle of friends, not only had the muscles of an occasional but strenuous weightlifter, he also had the weight of a voracious and unceasing eater. He was a man mountain, and right then he was sitting square on top of Dunn.

The instant they hit Dunn, Frank quickly moved to grab the detonator as it squirted from Dunn's hand.

Then he asked his friends, "Have any trouble with the goons guarding the house?"

"Naw," Chet said, getting off Dunn and letting him join his wife and sons against the wall. All four of them had their hands raised. "Those guys were too busy looking at the house to see us coming up from behind. We tied them up real nice for delivery to the cops."

"Well, keep these guys on ice while I go get Callie," said Frank.

By now Dunn had found his voice. It came out in a snarl. "So you set a trap for me, Hardy."

"Now you're the one who's being a bright boy," said Frank with the relish of revenge.

"Sure, I see it all now," said Dunn, nodding his head as rage smoldered in his eyes. "You wanted to make sure you could get your hands on me so I would tell you where Callie is. You figured I was the big cheese, and once you had me, it would be easy to mop up everything else."

"Good thinking," Frank said.

"Too bad yours isn't as good," said Dunn. "I hate to break the news. But you're not going to find sweet Callie out in the driveway. That thing's a dummy, a bluff. I just didn't want any shooting till I was in control. And besides, I'm not even the boss on this operation. He's the one who's going to pull the trigger on your sweetheart."

Frank's mouth was a thin, hard line as he digested the news. He walked to the front and looked out the window, hoping to prove Dunn a liar. When he returned he said, "I may not know much, but I do know who'll pull the trigger on you if you don't tell me where Callie is."

Dunn just smiled. "Come on, Frankie boy, I know you too well to buy that."

"You're wrong, Dunn," Frank said menacingly. "And you don't want to find out how wrong. Shooting you would be like shooting a poisonous snake."

But Dunn kept smiling. "Nice try, but I don't bluff."

Frank stood, staring for a moment at Dunn, then shrugged in defeat. "Hold this, will you?" he said to Walter Rawley, and handed him the gun. Then he faced Dunn again. "You're right, I couldn't use a gun on you, but"—he extended his hands and flexed them purposefully—"I can do things with *these* that might make you prefer the gun." He paused and looked straight into

146

Dunn's eyes. "Are you sure you want to find out how far I'll go to rescue Callie?"

"Oldest trick in the world—hiding someone in a place you've already searched," Frank said to Joe. They were moving cautiously toward the bungalow where they had found William Clark's corpse.

"Yeah," agreed Joe. "Pretty good idea, though. With Clark out of the way, it's a real safe spot to stow somebody."

The Hardys had left John Dunn and his fiendish family under the guard of Walter Rawley, Biff, and Chet. Frank said that as soon as Joe and he got Callie back safe and sound, they'd phone and the cops would be called in to haul the Dunns away.

John Dunn said that Callie had been left alone in the bungalow, bound and gagged, but the Hardys were taking no chances.

"No way we're betting our lives, not to mention Callie's, on that slimy character's telling the truth," Frank said.

Joe nodded. "That guy lies as naturally as he breathes. Which way do you want to bust into the bungalow?"

"Let's give them a one-two punch," Frank said. "I'll go around to the back door and pick the lock. Give me four minutes to do that. Then you ring the front doorbell. I'll wait thirty seconds, then skip inside. If anybody but Callie is in the house, we'll have him in a pincer.''

''But what if somebody inside takes a look at me through the peephole?'' asked Joe.

''The door doesn't have one,'' said Frank. ''I noticed that the first time we were here. I remember thinking that Clark had no way of knowing that a killer had come knocking on his door.''

''You don't miss much, do you?'' Joe grinned. ''Got to admit, it does come in handy sometimes. Let's synchronize our watches.''

It took Frank only a couple of minutes to pick the back-door lock. Fenton Hardy had given both him and Joe instruction in this skill, saying that if the two were going to be detectives, they'd have to know how to get through locked doors of all kinds. Fenton knew what he was talking about.

Frank watched the numbers on his digital watch flashing until it was time for him to move, and when it was, he moved fast.

He went through the door quickly, ready to battle anyone who might try to stop him. But the coast was clear in the kitchen. Still on guard, he moved into the next room, and relaxed.

There was only one person in it.

Callie.

She was in a chair, bound and gagged, just as Dunn had said.

Frank relaxed, weak with relief.

"Callie, you're okay," he said, and moved toward her.

But as he came closer, he saw she was rolling her eyes, as if desperately trying to tell him something, warn him of something.

He glanced around, saw nothing, and hastily took the gag from Callie's mouth.

"Watch out, he'll be back in a second!" she gasped.

" 'He'?" said Frank.

But before she could answer, there was a crash from the next room.

And then Joe's voice.

"Call me ghostbuster!"

When Frank reached the next room on the run, he saw the answer in front of him.

It was lying practically where he had seen it before.

The body of William Clark.

This time, though, there was one big difference. Frank had time to see that it was breathing.

"I don't know who was more surprised when he answered the door, him or me," Joe said an hour later, after the police had come and picked up Clark and the Dunns at Callie's house. Joe and Frank were sitting with Callie and Walter Rawley, tying up the last threads of the web of deceit. "I recovered first, though," Joe went on, "just in time to cool him before he could get his gun out."

"That's what happens when a crook gets away with too much for too long," said Frank. "He gets overconfident. Clark must have been so sure Mr. Rawley and you and I were already wiped out that he felt safe in answering the door."

"He was confident, all right," said Callie. "So confident that he figured he didn't even need to keep me alive. He forced me to write a supposedly secret note that John Dunn would pretend to find implicating Mr. Rawley as a murderous master spy. He said that Fenton Hardy would be stunned enough by the death of his sons not to question that evidence. He paid me the compliment of saying that I was too smart for my own good, and that he'd feel safer with me out of the picture."

Walter Rawley shook his head. "It's still hard to believe. Meek, mild, loyal William Clark. He's been with me long—ever since I started Laser."

"And he's been stealing secrets all that time," said Frank. "He's the big boss that Dunn was talking about. He's the one who decided that your company was so big now that the only way to have access to everything it was doing was to take it over completely. And he had to be the one who worked out the scam, the one who knew that the loss of your wife left you vulnerable to somebody like Linda."

"Come to think of it," said Walter Rawley, nodding, "he did keep urging me not to work so hard on the California business trip I took, the one where I met Linda. He said I should try to have a little fun, meet new people. I was really touched by his concern." He gave a grimace. "And I guess I was almost killed by it."

"Well, you're not the only one who was taken in," said Frank consolingly. "I have to admit I was almost fooled too."

"Almost," said Joe. "Come on, they practically had you jumping through hoops. All they had to do was make you want to prove to Callie that you could beat out Greg in finding the truth. You were so eager that you shut your eyes to anything that might slow you down."

Frank cleared his throat and hoped the something that felt very much like a blush wasn't coloring his face. "Well," he finally said, "it's true that I didn't want Callie to be taken in by a guy like Greg. Not that I was jealous, understand. I mean, 'concerned' would be a better word. That's it, I was a little concerned."

Callie, who had been listening to this with a straight face, couldn't stop herself from smiling now. "You mean, I went to all that trouble to make you jealous, and it didn't work?"

"Then you really didn't think Greg was so hot?" said Frank, smiling too.

"What I did think was that maybe you've been taking me for granted lately," said Callie. "Going steady is one thing, but going to sleep on a relationship is something else. I figured you needed something to wake you up."

"Well, next time," Frank said, putting his arms around her waist, "send me an alarm clock."

Frank and Joe's next case:

Five years ago Denny Payson's father died in a fire at the chemical plant where he worked. Now Denny's eighteen, and he's out to get the man he claims is responsible for his father's death—Lucius Crowell, owner of the plant.

There's a problem though. Not only is Crowell a respected businessman, he's running for public office. No one believes Denny's charges. Frank and Joe decide to do some checking on their own. What they find is Crowell's dirty past, and they realize Denny is in serious danger. With Crowell's hired thug on their trail, the Hardys have to stop Denny before he makes one last, final move in *Line of Fire*, Case #16 in The Hardy Boys Casefiles.